HOMETAKER

BOOKS BY DEAN F. WILSON

THE CHILDREN OF TELM

Book One: The Call of Agon
Book Two: The Road to Rebirth
Book Three: The Chains of War

THE GREAT IRON WAR

Hopebreaker
Lifemaker
Skyshaker
Landquaker
Worldwaker
Hometaker

THE GREAT IRON WAR - BOOK SIX

HOMETAKER

DEAN F. WILSON

Cover illustration by Duy Phan

First Edition 2016

ISBN 978-1-909356-17-7

DIOSCURI PRESS

Published by Dioscuri Press
Dublin, Ireland

www.dioscuripress.com
enquiries@dioscuripress.com

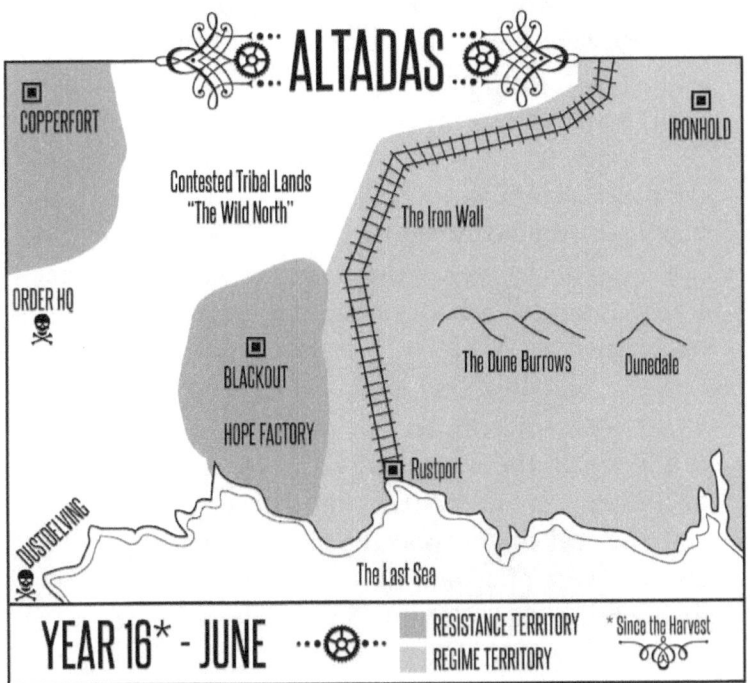

THE GREAT IRON WAR

In the world of Altadas, in the year 1888 of the Second Era, women everywhere dreamed of a coming desert. Those who were already pregnant miscarried, and those who became pregnant did not give birth to human children. An invasion had begun.

The newborns had no horns or marks, and so they were loved and reared like all the others. It would take time before anyone realised what they really were, before anyone would call them demons.

These events were marked by the arrival of strangers claiming to be from a distant land. The people of Altadas called them Pilgrims, but they did not know just how far they had come, nor by what strange doors they had entered, nor exactly what they had come for.

The first Pilgrims were scouts, but subsequent waves were soldiers, sent by a man who would later call himself the Iron Emperor. He promised his people iron. He gave them war instead.

They called that year the Harvest, and it became the first year of a new, darker calendar. Sand swept through the great chasms in the sky from where the demons came, the dust of a world that they had dried up. Ahead of the landships went great sandstorms, until the green grasses became an endless red desert.

In Altadas, steam powers industry, but iron powers war. The abundant metal, idolised by the invaders, and depleted in their home world, became a beacon to the demons, and was the foundation upon which they would build their new civilisation. They called themselves the Iron Empire. Their enemies simply called them the Regime.

As war began in the east, few among the Resistance knew that their own children were not really theirs. The invaders had mastered a magical technique to control the birth channels of a people they desired to conquer. Thus with one hand they would wield might, and with the other they would use guile, infiltrating and eradicating their enemies, anyone who would dare defy the Iron Emperor, who had brought his people to this promised land.

Yet iron is more to the demons than just a metal. It provides the key ingredient for the sustenance of the invaders. To some it is a drug. To them, symbolising everything they were promised, and everything they were leaving behind, it is Hope.

As one civilisation crumbled, and a new empire was founded on its remains, there were some who refused to live out their last days under the iron grip of their new ruler. They made a promise of their own: to fight, with everything they had, for the fate of humanity.

Thus began the Great Iron War.

CONTENTS

Chapter

Chapter One

SUB ROSA

Rommond planned to keep it quiet, but like with many of his plans—and plans in general—things did not work out that way. The Hometaker was such a big project, with so many parts, it required a lot of people to be involved, hauling Glass crystals and iron ingots from Fort Landlock, musing over Brooklyn's arcane instructions, and plotting what might happen if they pulled it off. A lot of people. A lot of voices. Someone was bound to talk.

"I want to know who," the general growled. "We need at least a month on this. We're barely a week in and tongues are already wagging."

The newly-promoted Lieutenant Myre stammered his response. "It's hard to t-tell who might—"

"Find them," Rommond barked. "Find them and silence them."

"Okay." The lieutenant straightened his uniform. At least that he could control. Yet adjusting it was a mistake, because it drew the general's attention to an unorthodox adornment hanging from his coat pocket.

"What's that?" Rommond asked, gesturing to the charm.

"My lucky gold coin."

"It isn't really standard attire, is it?"

"Well, no, but—"

"It sets you apart."

"Isn't that a good thing?" the youthful lieutenant said.

"Not in battle. If you stand out enough, then every gun will point your way."

"But with this, they'll miss."

Rommond grumbled to himself.

Newly-promoted, Jacob thought. *That's more like a demotion. Hell, a death sentence.*

Rommond laid his pistol down on the table, that now familiar gesture, and the lieutenant turned and left. It was a tidy retreat, the kind of neat stride that likely earned Rommond's eye when he was looking over who was up for a rise in rank. Not that the list was big. It was a sad state of affairs that one of the biggest selling points any soldiers had was: they were still alive.

"So," Jacob said, noting with a sense of irony that he was the last remaining in the room. He had earned the general's trust. How things had changed. *You know*, he thought, *he's earned mine as well.*

"Don't you have work to do?" Rommond replied. *He* certainly did. The bunker beneath Blackout was lined with maps and battle plans, and toy soldiers that made Jacob's heart pang a little. He remembered making ones just like it, back in the workhouses of his youth.

Jacob shrugged. "Can't say I'm much of an engineer or a battle planner."

"Well, you've got two good arms there, so you can help with the deliveries at least."

"I've already helped with that. They didn't quite *want* my help." The echo of the delivery overseer's reprimand still rung out in Jacob's ears: *go back to your war, soldier!* He was a "Blackout boy" through and through, but Blackout was changing swiftly all the time—changing hands and changing ways. It did not really dawn on the smuggler that maybe the real reason he did not feel he fit in there any longer was because he himself had changed much more.

"They didn't want your help?" Rommond asked, raising an eyebrow. He gave a wry smile, before returning his gaze to one of the maps, an outline of Regime territory. "I wonder why." He looked up again when he saw that Jacob had not left. "Maybe you can help Tardo with his communications gear. We'll need to be able to broadcast far and wide. I want to give the Baroness a tour of the new setup in the clock tower as soon as Tardo is finished with it. Should be quite a treat."

Jacob gave a small nod, then made for the door. He halted and turned around.

"Rommond," Jacob said.

The general sighed. "Yes?"

"Why isn't Taberah back yet?"

Rommond took a moment to respond. His moustache shuddered as his mouth worked silently beneath. "She's … busy."

"Too busy for this?"

Another uncustomary pause from one so invested in customs. "Too busy for much of anything," the general said.

Jacob looked to the floor, where he did not have to exchange eye contact as well as words. The general's eyes were very grim. Jacob wondered if his were too. He tried to remember Taberah's, and only saw that final look, that glance of goodbye. "I kind of got the feeling that maybe she mightn't come back."

Rommond pursed his lips and tapped his finger on the map before him. "We've got to focus on the work at hand."

"What's the end game here?" Jacob asked. It was hard to tell from the jumbled plans. Everything was in code and shorthand. He suspected there were some fake papers thrown in too—just in case. Rommond always kept his cards close to his chest. Sometimes you just never knew what he was planning. Sometimes Jacob wondered if even Rommond knew.

"The end game is ending this war," the general responded.

"Yeah, but how? What happens when the Home-taker is ready?"

There was no longer any hesitation in Rommond's voice. If the war had aged him, the war effort had made him young again, filled with the virility of necessity. He looked at Jacob with those same grim eyes, but now they were the eyes of grim determination.

"We take that pinprick portal out there and make it big enough for an army to march through. We're going to take back our world by taking theirs—and showing them just how bad the Iron Emperor really is."

* * *

When Jacob left, he bumped into Porridge, as gaudily dressed as ever in a sequinned red blouse with a floral scarf and hat, hauling a cart of scraps through the city. As soon as the trader saw the smuggler, he half-fainted onto his shoulder.

"Oh!" he cried. "I've been pulling on this for ages!"

Mustn't comment, Jacob thought.

"Thank God there's a strong man like you!"

"Ah," Jacob said. "You want me to do it?"

"Would you, dearie? Oh, thank you!" He pawed at Jacob's chest affectionately.

Doesn't look like I'm getting a choice.

He looked at the cart of belongings, while Porridge linked his arm. Most of the items were bits of metal, the kind of "doodads and doohickeys" the trader was known for.

"It's poor little Bitnickle," Porridge explained. "She didn't survive the crash."

"Sorry to hear that," Jacob said. "Eh, who's Bitnickle?"

"Oh, you've never seen a clockwork construct, have you, plum?"

"Oh," Jacob said. "One of those." His trip along the Rust Road was experience enough.

Porridge placed the back of his hand on his forehead. "Oh! It's just dreadful seeing her like this. I could just faint!"

"Yeah, well don't." Jacob pointed to a huge suitcase at the back of the cart, taking up half the space, and much of the weight. "What's that? Tools?"

"No, much more important!" Porridge shrieked. "That's my travel clothes."

"Pack light, huh?"

"I know," Porridge said solemnly, nodding. "I had to cut back."

"So," Jacob said, as he steered the cart over the cobblestones. "Why aren't you helping Brooklyn with … you know." He was not sure he should say it. Maybe Porridge did not know. It kind of seemed unlikely though, given they got some of the parts from him.

"Oh, that's much too arcane for me," Porridge said. "I'm more of an … experimenter. Just slap this on there, stick this in here, and … oh, who knows?" He fanned himself rapidly. "My approach is a little too haphazard for my dearest dandy, Rommond. I'm under strict orders not to touch a thing!"

"Funny that," Jacob said. "So am I."

Chapter Two

BEING BRAVE

Whistler spent the first few days of his recovery in his room, but boredom quickly overcame him, not to mention the feeling that he was not really safe. There were lots of guards there, but that was the room where he almost died. As much as the rope nearly suffocated him, he felt suffocated by being confined inside.

"Where are you going?" one of the guards asked for the umpteenth time when he tried to leave.

"Out."

"You can't go out."

"Why not?"

"The General's orders."

Not *doctor's orders*. The General's orders. He felt increasingly like Rommond's prisoner. The price of protection was getting to him. It seemed too high to pay.

He closed the door again, and heard the guard make sure it was firmly shut. He thought maybe he could make a dash for it, but there were guards all the way down the corridor, and on the stairs, and at the exit downstairs too.

He turned back to the room. They had removed

the rope, but he still felt its phantom grip around his neck. They removed the mirror in the room too, but he knew what he would see in it. He could see it faintly in the reflection of the window: the red marks fading into pink, but not fading altogether. They just added to the faint scars he already had. They say a zebra earns his stripes. A monster earns his scars.

He was not sure he had quite come to terms with what he was, but he was getting there. Meeting other "demons" helped, when they were good. Knowing he was not doomed to become evil, no matter what he wanted. Knowing they had a choice, that *he* had a choice. He only hoped the blood in him that came from Taberah was stronger than the blood that came from Domas.

The loneliness gave him lots of time to dwell and think on this. He had frequent visitors at first, but that died down quickly. They were all working on something—something big—but they would not tell him what it was. He heard one of them quip that he was too loose-lipped to know. He was offended, but he knew he should not be, because it was true. And yet, he felt like having someone to listen, like Jacob, meant he did not need to talk so much, hoping someone—anyone—would hear.

Jacob visited often, and argued with the guards outside, and joked with Whistler about them once he got past. He came up with names for all of them, and embarrassing stories about them that the boy knew were not really true, but they cheered him up all the same.

Then the smuggler left, and the boredom and

loneliness set in again. Whistler heard the city at work. He could feel it too. He wanted to look out of the window, but every time he approached, he felt a sudden panic, and had to back away. He wondered if he would ever be brave, like Jacob, like Rommond, if he would ever really become a man.

He wondered, too, why his mother had not visited yet.

Maybe she's busy, he thought. Of course, she always was. Everyone was.

Another day would pass, and another thought would be discarded upon the pile of thoughts he had gathered the days before, like his own mental scrapyard.

Maybe she's coming now.

He waited by the door for her, listening to the chatter of the guards outside.

Maybe tomorrow.

He knew he was lying to himself, but then he had lied to himself in the cell of the Hold when he met Jacob and told the smuggler: "They're coming. They're supposed to come. They'll be here." He did not really believe it then, but it was true. There was still a kind of hope that was not poison.

She's coming, he told himself. *She's supposed to come. She'll be here.*

Another day passed, and the city's chatter changed. He could never quite make out what the people said, because so many people said it, but all those different voices, and different comments, united into one great voice, the voice of the city itself—and it sounded disturbed.

Curiosity must have been the bedfellow of courage, for he felt it well up inside him and propel him towards the window, where his focus on the crowd outside overcame any sense of fear he had before. He did not remember the evil night of a week ago. His attention was stolen by the mob that brayed after a man being hauled by soldiers through the streets, a man who looked very much like Gregan, yet a lesser man from this distance, perhaps made lesser by his actions.

Whatever terror Whistler had felt that night, when he thought and felt that it all would end, and struggled desperately against it, melted away at the sorry sight of the bedraggled and beaten man they dragged along the cobblestones, tripping and falling and stumbling, his clothes covered in stains from the rotten fruit that the crowd catapulted at him. He had grown an ugly, unkempt beard, and his hair was a mess. From such a vantage point, whatever strength he had a week before seemed vanished. From that distance, those great big arms and hands looked small.

As the crowd continued to hurl insults—which were just as rotten, and, more importantly, free—Whistler wondered if they hated the man because of what he did, or because of what he was. Were they a demon crowd that hated a human? Or were they a human crowd that hated the demonic act? He could not make out their words. He thought maybe some of them did not even know what Gregan did, or why they were there. Others walked, so they walked. Others marched, so they marched. Others hurled, so they hurled.

He watched as they dragged Gregan to the city prison, a place once emptied to bolster the dwindling forces of the Resistance. Some crimes were forgiven to fight a greater crime. Or maybe it was just more efficient to send the criminals to the front line. Yet now that the prospect of the war ending was passing from tongue to ear like the plague, it seemed time for sophistication once more, time once again for lock and key.

Then, glancing back at the closed door behind him, Whistler climbed out of the window and down the frame of the Olive Inn, carefully avoiding the guards below. He abandoned his own prison and headed towards the one where Gregan was locked up, intent on confronting the man who tried to kill him, hoping to understand why, and fearing he might never know the answer.

Chapter Three

THE NIGHT OF NOTHING

There were many councils called to discuss the upcoming manoeuvre, what the Resistance hopefuls were calling "the final battle," and what the Resistance pessimists were calling by the same name in a much more despondent tone. Most meetings excluded any turncoats from the Regime, but Jacob encouraged dialogue, and Rommond arranged a token discussion in his bunker to give the Regime rebels a sense of being involved.

"Trust is earned," the General warned the smuggler, "but turncoats earn trust too, before turning it like a blade upon those too trusting. There's only one thing to trust wholeheartedly: your doubt, your suspicion, the surety that you can *always* be betrayed."

"All the more reason to get them involved," Jacob responded, "to keep them close."

"And our enemies closer?"

Jacob grinned. "Close enough to kill them."

"Well then," Rommond said with a smile, "let's reel them in."

* * *

The token meeting saw the bunker crammed with the top brass of the Resistance, all in a show of camaraderie with their compatriots from the opposing side. There were maps and battles plans on show, rather brazenly even, but Jacob noted with a little humour that they were very different to the ones he had seen before. He wondered if even he was only privy to the fakes, if the general put on a different show for each and every person allowed to enter his bunker.

Trust only your suspicion, the smuggler thought. He could not blame the general's caution.

The meeting went well, and if anyone there really did doubt the other, they did not show it.

"We need everyone," Jacob said. "There's been enough death and destruction 'round here."

Trokus nodded. "There has. And this war isn't over yet. You've yet to meet the Iron Emperor. You'll think the death and destruction you've seen so far is nothing when you face him."

"Why did you fight for him?" Jacob asked.

"Fear," Trokus said. "Fear for my family. And duty. Duty for my people. But you don't know him like we do. To many, he's this far-off symbol. He's so high up, he's almost a god. You demonise him. We deify him. And maybe at the end of it all, he's just a man. But if you've never met him, it's easy to say that. Anyone who meets him is *changed* by him."

"Did you meet him?" Jacob wondered.

"No, but one of my brothers' did, and he became a fanatic after that. And one of my closest friends did, one I'd known since I was but a child, and he went from wanting to start an uprising to wanting to crush the Resistance. They say you can't even look him in the eye, or he changes you. So most of us just keep on going, looking after our own, hoping to stay out of the spotlight."

"Then your own start vanishing off the streets," Rommond said.

"So you heard of that."

"The Night of Nothing," the general said.

"We have other names for it. It was pretty clear the next day when only the dissenters disappeared. Who knows where they are now, if they're even still alive. I shouldn't even be talking about this. I vowed, for my family, to just keep quiet. But I can't help but think that one day, they'll come for us too."

"What happened?" Jacob asked.

"It was in the first year of the war, when all the Iron Emperor's promises turned to ash. Many rebelled against him, and there was a growing movement forming to oust him from power. They were known as the Blinders. They sealed up their own eyes to stop the Iron Emperor's controlling gaze, and they sought to blind him, so that he could never control people again. It started small, but it grew rapidly, especially with those far from Ironhold, far from the Iron Emperor's reach."

"What happened to them?"

"We don't know, but I can only imagine they were slaughtered."

"Alex brought me to Black Fields," Brooklyn interjected, "where people are left to die."

"That was later," Trokus said. "The Black Fields are for today's malcontents. Yesterday's were much more numerous, too many for the Black Fields to hold."

"Black Fields seemed vast to me."

"They are, but you really don't understand how much dissent there was early on. He promised us a perfect land. He promised us a cure. He promised an end to war and violence. He promised to restore the balance of all things. All he did was deliver more death and disease. By the end of the first year, some estimated the Blinders had grown to maybe a hundred thousand."

"Hell," Jacob said. "That should've been enough to overthrow him, no?"

"It should have," Rommond grumbled. "We've never even had those numbers."

"Yes, and they were poised to strike," Trokus continued. "Poised to blind. But they were blind themselves. They didn't know that the Iron Emperor let them grow, let them show who among his people could not be trusted. And then, just a week before their planned operation to oust him, he implemented his own secret plan. The Night of Nothing. First, all the power went out. We were plunged into darkness. People tried to hide, but the Iron Emperor had a secret force ready to seize everyone even remotely suspected of supporting the Blinders. I lost many of my family then. I was lucky I didn't lose my wife. She cared nothing for the Iron Emperor, but I pleaded with her not to show it, and never to act on it. We think now that it was the Iron Guard he used, but we still don't know where they took the people."

"That's pretty grim," Jacob said. "I can't blame

you just putting your head down then."

"Maybe it's not the right choice, or the just choice, but it's the one we made to survive. When the Night of Nothing was over, those hundred thousand people were gone, and so were thousands more who were suspected of being sympathisers. It took a year for that dissent to grow, and in a single night the Iron Emperor plucked them out like little more than weeds. In a single night, the chance of rebellion was crushed."

"Let's see what a single day will do then," Rommond said.

Chapter Four

IRON BARS

Whistler tucked his tell-tale tangles into his cap and hid himself amongst the crowd. He had learned a lot from Jacob. A smuggler of things was also a smuggler of people, even if it was just himself. He mingled with the mob, copying their chants, mimicking their movements.

"We've had enough war!" one of them shouted as they congregated outside the prison.

"Can't even trust our own!" another barked.

"Child-killer!" a third spat, firing the spittle towards Gregan as he was hauled towards the prison door.

Whistler was still alive, so he did not think the last claim was entirely accurate, but for the purpose of his little mission, he thought it best if he play dead.

Gregan did not protest. It looked like he might have done before, when he was first caught, but he had the bruises to show that protesting did not do him any good. Squelched tomato still dripped from his face and hair. The guards seemed to loiter at the prison door far longer than they needed to, just long enough for the angry crowd to get in another throw.

Then Gregan was hauled inside, into what must

have then seemed like the safety of the cell. The crowd continued to yell and holler for a time, and the walls of the prison were now the target of their throwing arms. Whistler felt unsettled by the madness of it all, but he mouthed the insults all the same, and when he was handed a rotten apple, he lunged it half-heartedly at the bricks and mortar. The walls did nothing to him.

The fruit ran out before the insults did, but soon they too died down. It seemed it just was not the same when the crowd could not see their target's reaction. They came to boo and shame. They needed to see the red cheeks of the shameful, or make them red with tomato juice. The people, united in this moment of condemnation, began to disperse, back to their separate segments of the city, leaving Whistler exposed again.

It was then, in that moment of panic, that he remembered one of Jacob's smuggling routes, all of which he had made the smuggler teach him with as much precision and attentiveness as he gave to Jacob's first lesson on decorum with his spoons. There was another way into the prison, part of the underground network of tunnels that Rommond was now using to work the war effort. While the general had sealed off some of these, to prevent what he called "the riff-raff," Whistler was almost certain that the one leading from the old butcher's shop to one of the cells was still in operation. He just had to hope that was not the cell they put Gregan in.

Whistler disappeared into the city smog, which gathered at knee height, bumping into people regularly, being pushed and shoved, and finding he had to push and shove in turn if he was to get anywhere. He did not like Blackout, and wondered how on earth it had produced someone as kind as Jacob, so gruff in appearance, and so gentle beneath.

Eventually he found his way to Raw Royce's, the old butcher's shop. It had a different name before, but the population of Blackout had changed a lot. Now it was run by Royce, a balding, rose-cheeked man in a blood-speckled apron. A *demon*, Whistler noted, with that skill he once did not understand why he had, and once thought useful. Now it did not matter if someone was human or maran. They could still be fighting on either side.

"Half a pound for momma dearest, boy?" The butcher greeted him with a smile.

"Eh, no. I, uh, was wondering if I could use … the tunnel."

"The tunnel? Whatever for?"

"Just, like, to play in."

"Not much good playing down there, boy. Sure, it's full of vermin!"

"I was … hoping to catch a pet."

"A pet!" the butcher shrieked. He hammered his cleaver through a piece of meat. "Those aren't the types for pets. You should visit Ivory Tom in the Gold Quarter if you've got some coils to spare, which by the looks of you, you don't. He's got some fine specimens there, though there's not much demand for pets nowadays. He's only still in business because the Treasury still is, and they still want their fineries, so they do. But me, well, I'll always be in business, because people love their meat, come rain or shine, or shine and shine, as the case may be!"

"I've always wanted a mouse," Whistler said. It was not wholly a lie. Uncle Alex had one when he was little, and it was an adorable creature, scurrying around the dig sites, helping in those small discoveries.

"Can't say I understand why," Royce said. He scrunched his mouth up, working it around visibly as the cogs of his mind worked, gestating the notion. "All right then, boy, but if you don't find one in half an hour, you get back out here and go back home if you have one."

Whistler disappeared into the back of the butcher's, catching the man's final words: "And don't pick a rat! No one likes a rat!"

The tunnels were dark, lit only by the faint glow of oil lamps dotted very far apart. They were kept alight as part of the protocols of war, so that the Treasury members could escape the city. Rommond was as keen as ever that those protocols were kept in place.

Whistler scurried through the passage as quickly as he could. As much as he hated the awful scalding of the sun, he did not like the cold and the dark that Jacob seemed to prefer. He did not want to hide. He supposed that was more of his mother's blood in him. Maybe they were not so far apart after all. He found himself musing a lot on that lately.

In time he found the rusty ladder that led to a hatch into the prison above. The hatch was heavy, and the rust had almost welded it shut. There were many times when he wished for physical strength, for his boyish arms to be replaced by the muscle and sinew of manhood. This was one of them. It took his whole weight to make the hatch door budge. He remembered one of Rommond's sayings: "Put your shoulder into it, boy, and the rest of you will follow. Shoulder first." It was no wonder that the general called his most elite platoon the shoulder of his army. Yet they were gone now. Sometimes the sayings were just sayings, just words.

When the hatch was fully opened, Whistler scampered up, finding himself in an open cell right next to Gregan's. It was just the two of them. No other prisoners. No guards.

Gregan almost leapt out of his skin. "Blimey, boy. You almost killed me."

Whistler glowered at him, his dust-covered hair in his eyes. "Wouldn't that be fair?"

Gregan gave the faintest chuckle. "Would've thought you'd had enough of me."

Whistler did not respond to that remark. He had enough of the violence and hate, for sure. He had not had any of the answers. That was why he was there.

"I just wanted to know," Whistler said, shaking the dust from his hair. "Why?"

"Why what?"

"Why did you try to kill me?"

"You're one of *them*."

"But I'm not."

"Yeah, I suppose you're worse."

"How?"

"You're the blurring of the lines."

"I don't understand."

"You're what happens when they mix with us. We

end up with 'people' like you, a bit of both. Can't tell what part of you came from where. Can't tell your allegiance. It's all a blur."

"Isn't that a good thing? Like, to heal our differences?"

Gregan laughed. "You don't heal that, boy. You keep scratching that scab till it peels off, till it shows the ugliness underneath. See, you demons talk about your disease, your search for a cure, but you're the disease. And you, boy, you half-breed, are the evidence that we're infected. Humanity's been pushed to the brink, but screw it, I don't want to save it if I'm saving half of them as well."

"I don't get it," Whistler said. "You'd rather we all die?"

"Better than the demons living."

"But what if we all can live?"

"Not while I have any say. It's them or us. Well, I say 'us', but you ain't included in that."

"But you don't even *know* me."

"Doesn't matter. There's enough of them in you. That's all I need to know."

Whistler shook his head. "It doesn't make any sense."

"Give up, boy. You can't save everyone."

"No," Whistler said. "I don't care what you say. I don't care if you hate me. I'm going to keep trying. My mom always told me to keep trying, to keep fighting, to keep—"

"Your mom's dead," Gregan said.

Whistler halted mid-breath. "No."

"She's dead. She's been dead for days."

The boy shook his head, scattering the dust. "You're lying."

Gregan smiled. "Did no one tell you?"

Whistler faltered. He pushed the unlatched door of the cell open and made for the door, back into the light outside, where the sun revealed many things, but did not reveal his mother's passing. "She's dead," he heard Gregan calling from inside. The door slammed shut, and it felt like it slammed on his heart.

Chapter Five

THE LOSS-MAKERS

"So," Rommond said, sitting down before his lieutenants, "who tells him?"

The silence answered that question well enough.

"I must have told thousands of families by now," the general mused. "It almost doesn't mean anything any more. And from me, it must come across as insincere. *Miss, your son is dead.* Followed by: *Have you got another son of fighting age?* Because to me, it's a loss of soldiers, a loss of infantry. I have to plug that gap. I am a loss-maker, and I only hope that I make greater losses on the other side."

"Isn't the smuggler close to the boy?" one of the lieutenants suggested.

"Yes," Mudro said. "But we haven't told him either."

"The funeral's in just a few days."

"That's why we're having this conversation now," Rommond said.

"Have we not maybe left it a little late?"

"He's been through enough, that boy."

"Haven't we all? We can't protect people from death."

"I'm not sure I have enough heart left to break,

and I think I'd need a lot to tell that child. He's still starry-eyed, still sees the good when it's buried by evil, still has the cheer when it's swamped by sorrow. I've killed a lot of people in this war. I'm not sure I can kill what's left of his innocence."

"I think Jacob has to break the news," Mudro said. "But we need to break it to him first. He was close to Taberah too. They lost their child together. I think you're going to have to deliver that news, Rommond. I think it means more if it comes from you."

The general made no more delay, asking around for Jacob, finding he was much more difficult to pin down than he expected.

You're always around when I don't want you, he mused to himself. *And now that I do, you're nowhere to be seen.*

He found him eventually in one of the other inns that dotted the city. *The Horse and Hook*, run by Cameron Hamhart, a tall fellow with a distinct chinstrap beard, and one who was never seen out of his bear-stained sleeveless undershirt. It seemed Jacob had worked up quite a tab at the Olive Inn, and Gus was no longer willing to serve him. It was not the least bit surprising to find him at a bar.

Good, the general thought. *You'll need a drink.*

"Jacob," he called out, finding the smuggler slumped on the counter.

"I helped Tardo," Jacob said quickly, seemingly feeling the need to explain himself. "I'm on a break. Everyone's got to have a break."

"Indeed," Rommond said, tapping his finger at

Jacob's empty whiskey glass. "Some even eat when they're at lunch."

"Just whetting my appetite."

"With some neck oil?"

"Got to keep the gears in good order."

"Indeed." Rommond nodded to Hamhart, who smiled in return. "A sherry for me. I presume another whiskey for him."

Jacob gave a thank you, mid-hiccup.

"Seems you're already more than a little inebriated."

"You mean sloshed?"

"Quite."

Jacob shrugged. "Not much else to do around here."

"I had hoped to find you in a better state," the general said, "but maybe there's not really a better state for this." He fired a coil across the counter towards the barman, which Jacob caught mid-slide.

"Funny, huh?" he said, seemingly not registering any of Rommond's words. He turned the coil around in his hands, settling on the image of the Iron Emperor, with his colour-changing eyes. "How a man can do so much damage. And here we are, hic, drinking to him."

"Not *to* him, certainly."

"Because of him, then."

"Those days are ending," Rommond stated, grasping the glass of sherry the barman just filled. He usually grasped guns.

"Are they?"

"Hopefully."

Jacob flicked a smile off his lips just like he flicked the coil. "Hope."

Rommond buried his sigh in his glass, swamping down the lot and pointing to the glass when he got the barman's attention once again. Hamhart filled it up once more, closer to the brim, which he charged extra for, and gave a smile for free. Jacob barely touched his own glass.

"Jacob, what I have to tell you isn't easy."

The smuggler did not move. He kept his attention on the Iron Emperor's visage, as if he had been caught in that controlling stare.

When Rommond was about to utter the evil words that haunted him, Jacob spoke: "I know."

The general was caught off guard, something he was not used to, and it unsettled him. "You know?"

Jacob turned slightly to him, just enough to see his teary gaze. "I can feel it."

Rommond pursed his lips. It was even harder to say it now.

"She's gone, isn't she?" Jacob said, turning the coil around, face down, and placing it on the counter.

Rommond hung his head. "Yes. She's gone. She fulfilled her mission. But now..." He trailed off, turning back to the reassurance of the glass, which masked the tremor in his hand.

"How many of us do you think will survive this?" Jacob asked. "We've lost so many already. I sometimes wonder if we've used up all our luck. There's only so many times you get to cheat death."

"Jacob, if humanity survives this, I'll be happy," Rommond replied, "even if you only see my smile from the afterlife."

"So," Jacob said, "how do we tell Whistler?"

Rommond bit his lip. "I was rather hoping you would."

"Hell," Jacob said. "Guess I better sober up then."

No matter how many mugs of coffee he downed, Jacob still felt unsteady on his feet, and not quite steady in mind either. He dreaded the thought of telling Whistler the awful news, but thought that maybe the boy knew it in his heart just like he did.

Jacob wandered through the streets, stumbling every now and then, straightening himself up, dusting himself off, and feigning as much dignity as he could muster. He wondered if he should sleep it off first, but he felt compelled to tell the boy now, to get it over with. He might not have the courage in the morning when he was sober.

He made his way towards the Olive Inn, where he knew Whistler was still walled up, locked away from his attacker, and locked away from what everyone else knew outside. Then, as he turned a corner, Jacob thought he saw the boy walking slowly through the fog. Jacob closed his eyes tight, thinking it was the drink, but when he opened them again, there Whistler was, across the way, with only the ground-hugging smoke between them, like the spectral mist that clings to a grave.

He halted, and the boy halted. They saw each other through the haze, even through their own respective hazes of alcohol and tears. The other people of the city came and went, passing by them and between them, passing through the smog like spectres of their own. They only saw each other, and only thought of the third person that once united them, even if they never truly felt connected to her.

Jacob tried to communicate as much of his concern and sorrow and comfort in his eyes. And for the first time since he had met him, the boy turned away from him, back to the wandering, isolated road, back to the smothering of the smog.

"Whistler!" Jacob shouted after him. "Wait!"

The boy turned back, slowly, still dazed, still overcome. The sunlight reflected off the glisten on his cheeks, and in the water of his despondent eyes. It pierced the smoke, revealing what the grey concealed, and yet it revealed in Whistler a face that was sere and sullen, as if all the colour in him had been sapped out. The russet of his hair, tangled like the gnarled roots of graveyard trees, now seemed more brown than red, and the smoke further killed the colour that the sun tried to imbue.

Jacob hurried over to him, and even as he did, Whistler started to break down. He reached his hands out, but he did not reach them out to Jacob. Maybe he reached out for his mother. He reached for nothing.

Jacob fell to his knees before him and tried to pull the boy close.

"Why didn't you tell me?" Whistler wailed. He bashed his fists on Jacob's chest. It barely hurt at all, physically, but it hurt a lot to see him like this, to feel what he felt, and be powerless to help.

"I didn't know," Jacob said.

Whistler repeated the rebuke, but weaker now.

"Why didn't you tell me?"

Jacob held him close, stopping his flailing arms. "I didn't know, kid. I swear. I didn't know."

The boy must have smelt the alcohol on his breath. Whistler could not drink it all away, like he could. *I'm not sure if that's better or worse*, Jacob thought.

Whistler sobbed into Jacob's shoulder, so much so that the smuggler could feel the wetness of his tears. He held back his own, which he naively thought he had drowned in his glass. He had to cry inside, where no one could see, behind the locked door of his heart.

"I thought maybe ..." But Whistler could not finish the words.

Jacob held him closer, tighter, giving him the hug that his mother never did. That he felt it now in her passing was perhaps the greatest tragedy.

"I thought ... maybe ..."

"I know," Jacob said. He really did. It was what he once thought too, and what he silently hoped might still be, until Rommond killed that hope with his arrival at the inn. *Maybe we could be a family*. It was not to be. Whatever fates had stolen Elizah from them had stolen her mother too. Now there was just Whistler and Jacob left. The smuggler had little room left for hope. It was now buried by the fear that the fates would come back for them too.

Chapter Six

FUNERAL

For many in the Resistance, funerals were not that common. Not because people did not die, but because people died so often. Most had to make do with a makeshift grave where they fell. Often their coffin was shrapnel or debris, and sometimes it was the bodies of half a dozen fellow soldiers, all fighting for the same cause, all dying for it too.

But this was different. This was Taberah's funeral. Even to those who did not like her, or did not agree with her, her life was a symbol. It meant something. Her death meant something too.

The procession was slow and sombre, led by Rommond and Whistler. To most, it seemed like the boy was holding together well since the news—on the outside. He was probably still in shock. He had not said much. He had not eaten much either. Likely he had not slept at all.

The general kept his reassuring hand firmly on Whistler's shoulder. He knew the overpowering sense of loss. He knew the need for support. He knew when someone was faking strength, because he had been faking it for many years as well. *Don't let them see you fall*, he had told the boy. Whistler did not answer him, but here he was, walking that dreadful walk, keeping that lip from trembling, not letting anyone see him fall.

The coffin was draped with a deep red cloth, almost as red as Taberah's own hair. Several soldiers hauled it up, then lowered it down as the procession reached the grave. They had to act quick. The wind was picking up, threatening to fill in the hole in the sand prematurely.

As Rommond took out a speech, unfurling the neatly folded paper, Whistler turned around, seeming lost, until he found Jacob in the crowd and hurried over to him. If it was any other time, he might have ran to his mother. Jacob placed both hands on the boy's shoulders, filling that gap left by Rommond. As the general glanced up from the page, he wondered— and hoped—that the smuggler could fill the gap left by Taberah as well.

"This is an evil day," Rommond began, "out of more than a decade of evils." He looked to Brooklyn, standing at the back of the crowd, his black hair growing a little, his face and clothes stained with grease and oil, his hands still clutching several tools. He could only spare a moment from his labour to pay his respects. Otherwise, Rommond's eulogy might be for all.

"In this war," the general continued, "many come and go, and I'm afraid to say that many go before I even learn their names. But we all knew Taberah. No matter how fleeting your encounter was," and he looked to Jacob now, "she left a mark."

The smuggler hung his head. In doing so, he

looked down to Whistler, who looked down to the dusty earth that was soon to be Taberah's new home.

"Her drive," Rommond said, "was unlike any other's. Her determination was unstoppable, like a fire that engulfs a forest, passing from tree to tree. That fire she passed onto us. And maybe, if we can keep it alight, and pass it on to others, then part of her will still live."

There were many nods among the crowd. Few had not felt the burn.

"What set her on this path is what set many of us. She experienced the loss that many women did during the Harvest. She experienced the pain that followed. Though it may at times have driven her to the edge, she did not let it destroy her. She used that pain to fuel her, to drive her towards that one great goal she had in mind: cutting the cord to the Birthmasters.

"It was her discovery, by pushing us beyond what we thought were our limits, that gave us the amulets, and that was her pet project for many years, until she finally destroyed the demons that stopped human women from given birth to human children. For that, it is not just us who need to thank her, but our children, and humanity as a whole."

The nods were fiercer. Some prayed. Some said silent thank you's.

"She was a fighter, right from the start. That made her an integral part of the Resistance. When others gave up and tried appeasement," and he looked at General Leadman now, who gave him a dirty look in response, "she kept on fighting, fighting the good fight, fighting for the big picture. She died as she lived, fighting. I was going to say that maybe, wherever she is now, she's still keeping up the fight. But she doesn't have to. Because she won."

If it were not a funeral, there would have been applause.

"The fight isn't over for the rest of us, but maybe it will be soon. Let Taberah's life, and her great sacrifice, be an inspiration to us. Let her success give us a new kind of hope, that we too can win this war. To the fight!"

He beckoned for Whistler to join him, and Jacob came too. He knew this part would be hard, even harder than before. *Don't let them see you fall.* The coffin was opened for one last farewell. Taberah was in a vibrant red dress, the kind she wore to impress, and the kind she looked clearly uncomfortable in. She looked more comfortable now, more peaceful, and maybe there was even the faintest of smiles on her lips. The tribulations of life were over, and she had many of them to contend with. At last, she was at rest. Rommond wondered if this was the only way he could earn the same.

When the funeral was over, the people dispersed quickly. There was no wake. There was no time for it. Everyone had to get back to work, preparing for the fights to come.

Lorelai brought Whistler off, and comforted him like a mother would, like Jacob did not really know how to. She might have been a so-called demon, but the smuggler mused that there was a bit of an angel in her. She saw pain, and she came running, hoping to mend the hurt. It did not matter what side. It did not matter what hurt.

Yet the pain of Taberah's parting stung deeper than Jacob wanted to admit, than even the scorpion sting of her rejection of him. He knew it was not personal. He was not even sure what it was about her that enraptured him. Maybe it was her passion, that ever-burning fire. He remembered his words to her, almost a year ago: *Whistler said my nickname should be Spider, but why is it that I feel like I've been caught in your web?*

There were no cobwebs on the gravestone that was hurriedly erected there. It was pristine stone, newly carved, with the words: *She fought the good fight. And won.*

Jacob was alone, and yet even then he could not muster the words of a prayer. There were no words for this, even though people had experienced it a thousand times before, even though they had written eulogies and sung funeral dirges. The living could only allude to what was happening. The real words, the real language—it came from the dead. No one wanted to hear it, and yet they heard it sooner or later. Sooner for many. Sooner for most.

Jacob was lost in his thoughts, and those dreadful alleys of the mind were evil ideas linger, when he thought he saw something out of the corner of his eye. He turned to see a whirling black object approaching from the distance. He might have flinched or recoiled, thinking the Regime had begun their latest onslaught, had he not felt a little dead inside. The object was a monowheel, a large landship-treaded wheel, inside of which sat a familiar figure in a long, dark blue coat. Nox. The Coilhunter.

The monowheel pulled up close, the tumultuous thrumming of its engine filling the cavities of Jacob's chest. The Coilhunter placed a large, buckled boot on the ground, leaning the vehicle with him. A ceremonious puff of smoke came from the exhaust in his mask, just as the last plume coughed from the exhaust at the back of the monowheel. The dust settled, and Nox kicked a support stand out from the side, letting the vessel's weight fall against it. It sunk a little in the sand as he got up. He sighed audibly.

"Am I late?" he asked.

"Didn't even know you'd been invited," Jacob said.

"I wasn't."

Jacob did not ask him how he knew. Word got out. Gossip seemed to travel on the winds, and live in every grain of sand. The Regime was probably issuing its propaganda: *The Scorpion's Last Sting. The Scorpion Is Dead.* They would leave out the part about the Birth-masters' demise, of course. Maybe they were now losing the war, but they could still win the information one.

"The funeral's over," Jacob said.

"It's never over," Nox said, shuffling up beside him. "You bury them forever in your heart."

Jacob paused. "Were … you close?"

"She struck a chord."

"Yeah. She has a way of doing that."

Nox stared at the tombstone. "She *had* a way."

"I still can't really believe it."

"It ain't right, is it?"

"No," Jacob said. He paused for a moment, feeling like he needed to say something else. He was not sure if he was supposed to be sad or comforting. "I guess that's war."

Nox eyed him coldly from beneath the brim of his hat. "Is it?"

Another agonising pause. "So, how close were you?"

"Not much. You?"

Jacob pursed his lips. "Not much." They looked at each other, sharing the words with their eyes, but it was Jacob who spoke them: "Not sure anyone was."

"She had a kid," the Coilhunter said, as if to ask what happened to him.

"Yeah. He's devastated. I can't really imagine what he's going through."

There was that same dead look in the Coilhunter's eyes. "I can," he rasped.

"Sorry."

"Why?"

Jacob shrugged. "For your loss."

"Sorry for yours," the Coilhunter replied. "But we didn't do it, did we? So, ain't no need for apologies here, boy. We gotta get 'em from those who did."

He reached into his pocket and produced a rolled-up poster. He let it unfurl with the snap of his wrist, and though the wind caught it and tried to take it away, the words and the image were clear. *Wanted*. And that familiar face from the front of every coil: the Iron Emperor.

Chapter Seven

CROWN

Rommond gave the Baroness Ebronah, head of the Treasury, a quick tour of the new clock tower communications rig, where Tardo worked, ate and slept, all in a desperate attempt to get it fully up and running in time for what the general cheerfully called "the big reveal." General Leadman insisted on accompanying them, and Rommond was certain this was to get an "in" with Blackout's current leader.

"Consider it done," the Baroness said as the tour concluded.

"I'm not pulling your arm, am I?" Rommond asked.

"You are," she replied sharply, "but I'm happy to donate."

"We can do a lot with that much money. As much rests on this as what we'll be doing out there in the desert. This'll be the home front. I hope you're up for it."

She seemed offended, looking down her pointed nose at him. "Don't you worry about me, Rommond. It's you that we should be worried about. You be careful out there."

"I'm not sure I can be," Rommond replied. "We'll

be moving deep into Regime territory. Deeper than we ever planned to go. To their home world. To what we often called in our propaganda 'Hell'. None of this is careful now. It's all about risk. Every step. Every inch we take. It either ends for them, or it ends for us. There's no longer any room for stalemate."

"I trust you, Rommond. I trust you can do this. You've got that fighting spirit. I saw it in you when you were young."

"Well, I'm not that young any more. In fact, I'm feeling rather rusty. If I were a landship, the engineers would have retired me by now. We're most in need of a younger model."

Ebronah scoffed. "Hardly. Experience is what matters here."

"You were a bit of a fighter in your own youth, if I recall. Are you sure you wouldn't fancy taking up a rifle one last time?"

She gave a regal chuckle, and her voluminous skirts shuddered with her mirth. "I'm afraid my wrists might crack were I to do that. No, I'm better suited as an ornament of sorts here in Blackout, a little trinket of the Treasury, an example to people of how to act, of what to aspire to. It'd be quite something for one of my line to be seen getting out the dungarees, as it were."

"That'd be a sight and a half."

"Rommond," she said, taking his hand. "If I have any power here, then let me exert it upon you with this final command: come back, and come back whole. Whether or not we win this, come back. And most especially if the Iron Emperor falls, come back and lead us, for we will be most in want of a leader then."

Leadman coughed. He had been rather silent throughout, and Ebronah barely looked at him. Rommond suspected that the other general was not aware of how little regard the Baroness had for the leader of Copperfort.

Rommond gestured to him. "I'm sure that mantle can fall to General Leadman."

Ebronah let out a rapturous cackle, which made Leadman's enormous frown almost a permanent feature on his face. "Oh, I needed that," she said. "I'm sure Mr. Leadman will find a place, without question, but the people know who's been leading us through this war, and who should lead us after. It can only be you, Rommond."

Rommond blushed. "Let us win the war first, before we worry about the aftermath."

"Really, Rommond? From the Master Planner himself? Dearest me, I expect you'll have given some thought to the aftermath. The world will be very different then."

The tour ended, and Ebronah returned to her ministerial duties, and the war of words that often played out in the battleground of the Treasury headquarters. The two generals remained, standing by the door of the clock tower.

"Rommond."

"Leadman."

"I didn't see you speaking up much about my leadership bid in there."

"I spoke."

"You whispered."

Rommond sighed. "You must be a little deaf from the trenches. Oh wait, you didn't really spend much time in them, did you?"

"What if you die in this?" Leadman probed.

"I expect I shall sleep a little sounder then."

Leadman rolled his eyes. "And what about me?"

"I expect you'll sleep sounder too."

"I mean, who *vouches* for me then?"

"Leadman, I can't make the people follow you. I can suggest that you would be a good politician, but it's up to them to vote for you."

"You know there won't be a vote at first. It's martial rule. They're going to look to you for that interim government."

"And I'll keep my promise," Rommond said. "But Leadman, you already had your chance at the crown. When General Camderhill died, the leadership of the Resistance would have passed to you. You abdicated by opting for appeasement. If the leadership went to me, it's not because I sought it. It's because I kept leading. If you want to re-earn the people's trust, then shine on the battlefield."

It did not help, of course, that Rommond would be fighting there too. Leadman would not only have to shine. He'd have to outshine Rommond as well.

Chapter Eight

THE KNIFE

Lorelai sat in the darkness of the Olive Inn, her hand cradling an empty glass. Gus had offered her a lantern, and another drink, but she refused. She needed to think, and it was easier to do it in the darkness, when she could focus on her thoughts.

There was no one else in the tavern. Even Jacob was not there. Everyone knew this was now part of Rommond's headquarters. It made them nervous, so they drank elsewhere. She supposed it should have made her nervous too. She wondered if that was why she wanted to be in the dark, away from those human eyes, those eyes that would look into her maran ones, and see a demon.

She took out a small round mirror from her pocket and instinctively inspected her make-up. She did not wear a lot, but her eyes were rimmed, and her lips were bright. There was a certain expectation of women in the Regime. If you did not abide by it, if you did not don the right colours, you stood out as a rebel. Those women who wore no make-up at all stood out the most, and usually paid for it with their lives. It did not matter what the job was, that she was a field nurse, just behind the soldiers on the front line. She was expected to follow orders, to abide by customs, to keep her head down.

She folded up the mirror and placed it back in her pocket, where she felt the small pouch of Hope. She got a refill recently. Deliveries were still coming into Blackout from the abandoned facility down south. The Resistance might have regained control, but now it was their responsibility to deal with that drug, that food, that fuel. She was now as dependent on them as she was on her old masters. At any moment they could withhold it, and she would wither away. She had no reason not to expect them to do it. They had done many of the things the Regime had done. Both sides were guilty of numerous crimes.

You're dwelling on this, she told herself.

Then, as if the fates wanted to distract her, she heard the creaking of the front door. She meant to step up, or cough, or bang her glass on the table, or otherwise make her presence known, but something stopped her. She heard the harsh footfalls of leather boots, the kind of militarised march of good soldiers, the kind that General Rommond would promote. They moved straight to the bar, accompanied by the chatter of their owners, who were oblivious to Lorelai in the shadows of the corner.

"We'll have earned this drink," one of the lieutenants said, banging on the counter.

"Might be able to retire," the other replied with a laugh, as if that notion was inconceivable.

"Well, why not? The war'll be over."

"Do you really think he'll do it? Break into *their* world?"

Lorelai perked up, but kept herself inside the shadows.

"No reason to doubt it," the first lieutenant said, slapping the counter again. "Brooklyn's hard at work. Some sort of missile launcher. More Glass than iron is what I heard."

"He's more Glass than iron himself," the second said with a grin. "At least in the head." He paused. "I heard tell they expect to find proof Old Iron isn't who he says he is."

"Who knows? They might just find dust. But maybe we can send those demons back."

"Send 'em to Hell," the other quipped.

"Wouldn't mind sending a few others while we're at it."

They laughed. On realising that Gus was not coming, the first lieutenant reached over the bar and grabbed a bottle of gin and two glasses. They left, laughing, and the silence of the tavern returned, but it brought many different thoughts to Lorelai's mind.

She sat there for a long time, dwelling on everything. *They're going to go to Mes Marana*, she thought. *But there's nothing for them there.* Yet she wondered what they might find, and worried about what it might expose. If they could find some dirt on the Iron Emperor, perhaps the war would end. She yearned for it to end, for the killing and the hurt to stop. But she feared what might happen if they failed, if they riled up the man without a name, who had risen to power after the Iron Plague took hold, and who had promised them a cure.

She stood up, clasping the glass still. She held it

up to the light, where it glinted. It was a different type of glass, the kind that did not trap light. She placed it down on the table gently.

She left through one of the side entrances, where a Resistance guard gave her a habitual nod. She kept going, through the dim, quiet street, following the mental map of the city she had made, past the infirmary where she stored her supplies, where she had treated so many, human and maran, fighting on either side of the war, or no side at all. She passed by an alley where Jacob and Whistler were helping to load up a wheelbarrow full of iron scraps, and she hurried more quickly so that they would not see her. She saw many labourers as she walked, and wondered where Brooklyn was, working on his new machine. She continued on until she saw the clock tower peering over the rooftops, and kept walking and turning corners until she approached that building's front entrance.

It was not as well-guarded as it perhaps should have been. Of course, not many knew what it was being used for now. This was one of Rommond's unplayed cards. As she entered, she wondered what other ones he had that she did not know about.

She headed up the stairs, spotting Tardo kneeling over an array of wires, his mop of sweat-laden blonde hair almost tangled amongst them. He looked up, startled.

"I need your help," she told him. "Do the radios work?"

"Yeah. I can get pretty much any channel you want."

"Can you show me?"

"Eh … sure."

Tardo abandoned his project and headed over to the many desks piled up with equipment. He got that same glazed look in his eyes as he faded off into a dreamy state as he worked. It made it easier for Lorelai, because he did not see her grabbing one of the heavy pieces of equipment and slamming it down on his head. He collapsed with a grunt, leaving a little pool of blood on the floor. She instinctively felt like helping, like stitching him up. But she had more important duties.

She adjusted the radios. She did not need him for that. She knew the right channel, a secret channel, known only by the Pilgrims, the first marans to visit a world—the scouts.

"Pilgrimage," she spoke into the microphone. "K-194 reporting."

"Your report?" a voice crackled back.

"They're making a new weapon."

"Details?"

"A missile launcher, using Glass."

"For what purpose?"

"To open a Rift."

"They can't."

"Trust me. I've lived with them. They're determined. They can."

"Why are you breaking cover now? Were you not instructed to wait?"

"They say they will find incriminating evidence on the Iron Emperor."

There was silence on the other end. The static

played out for a long time.

"Can you get us more intel?" the voice came eventually.

"I'll try."

"You need to do more than try. The stakes are too high."

"I'll find out where they plan to launch their attack, but it might be difficult to report back. Suspicions will be high here."

"It's too late for that, K-194. If your cover is blown, you know what to do."

The radio went silent. She dwelt on the silence for a moment. Then, as she looked at Tardo unconscious on the floor, she dwelt on something else: her code number: *K-194*. She had a codename to go with it: *The Knife*. She dug it in when you were not looking, and then twisted it too.

Chapter Nine

SCRAMBLE

They found Tardo the next morning, bruised and bloodied. He could not remember anything that happened the night before, and a test of his blood showed the presence of a memory-dulling drug known to be used by Regime spies, sometimes on themselves.

"The message," Rommond said, dragging a chair across the floor. "Who was it to?"

Tardo sat under a spotlight, but it was the glare of the general's eyes that made him sweat. The room was sealed off. It was just him and Rommond in there. That was enough. That was too much.

"I don't know," Tardo replied. "I don't remember anything."

"Convenient, that."

"Not really. Not for me."

"You know what, Tardo. You're right. You see, I like answers. Clear, honest answers. Even if they're answers I'll hate. I like that I'll know them. What I don't like is being in the dark. What I don't like is having people around me I can't trust."

It was hard to see the demon in Tardo. He was quite young, and had that youthful vigour that

Rommond had seen in so many new recruits. It was usually the older ones he had to worry about. The young often died before they could learn to betray.

"You can trust me, General. I … I really just—"

"It was set to a new channel," Rommond interrupted, pointing his gloved finger to the radio equipment. "One we don't recognise. It doesn't even seem like that channel was ever used before. But we know a message was transmitted. We just don't know what it was. It seems there was some form of encryption used. That's your area, isn't it?"

Tardo looked dumbfounded. "Well, *I* don't know—"

"Because you took the drug."

"*What* drug?"

"The drug in your system, the one designed to stop you spilling the beans in the event we torture you."

"T-t-torture me?"

"Torture a spy."

Tardo shook his head frantically. "I'm not a spy, Rommond. I swear! I always wanted to be part of the Resistance. I never would—"

"Take him away," Rommond said to the nearby guards.

Tardo was dragged outside and hauled through the streets. It was night, so the streets were quiet, and no one knew yet of Tardo's alleged treachery. There might have been a mob for that too. It was easy to work up the crowd.

Tardo was given his own cell. As the metal door slammed shut, the sound woke up the man in the cell beside him. Gregan. He wiped the sleep and shock from his eyes, then smiled.

"Well, what do you know?" he said.

Tardo did not answer.

Gregan's grin widened. "Seems you're not all sweetness and nice after all."

"I was framed," Tardo protested.

Gregan laughed. "Weren't we all?"

In Rommond's bunker, the general sat alone, his chest still heaving, his fists still clenched. This was why he played his cards close to his chest. It seemed he could not trust anyone. So much rested on secrecy, on giving them the time necessary for Brooklyn to finish his work. He was still a ways off yet. He could not even say how many more days it would take. Maybe it would be weeks.

There was a sudden loud banging on the door.

"General, we have a visitor," a muffled voice said.

"Tell them to wait," Rommond replied. "I'm busy."

"You'll want to see them, General."

Rommond did not hide his angry sigh. He covered up his new maps and plans and left the bunker, which he locked behind him. At one time he wondered if he was being paranoid. Now he knew he was not being paranoid enough.

Outside, he found one of his own spies, one who orchestrated a constant cat and mouse chase of hacks against the Commspire network, gleaning momentary bits of intel before the security holes were swiftly patched up. They called him Codex Carter, and even with Rommond he wore a headscarf to hide his exact identity.

"General," he said, with a salute.

"Codex."

"We intercepted something."

"Hopefully our missing message."

"Not quite, but it won't take a genius to figure out what it was."

"Oh?"

"They know about the missile launcher. Someone had to tell them."

Rommond tried to hold back his angry sigh. *Tardo*. He should not have even known about it, but tongues were wagging everywhere. There were too many fresh-faced soldiers, lacking discipline.

"It's worse than that, Rommond."

"What do you mean?"

Codex handed him a stack of papers, all containing documented messages. "They're mobilising everything, General. It's really the only reason we intercepted anything in the first place. Their radios are in overdrive. There are orders going back and forth all day. They're barely even trying to hide it."

"And it's not a ruse? A bit of Mudro in them?"

"No," Codex replied. "We thought that too, but the scouts report that the mobilisation is real. This is larger than anything we've seen. It seems they're emptying the barracks for this."

"What's their plan? Where are they mobilising to?"

"To the Rift, Rommond, the doorway to their world. And they're going to get there before you.

When you arrive, it seems the door will have a *lot* of guards."

Chapter Ten

PROJECT THIMBLERIG

With the Regime mobilising, and Brooklyn's design far from complete, the Resistance had to get mobile too. The problem, as many saw it, was that they were just becoming a moving target. They were still a target all the same.

Rommond spent a lot of time with Doctor Mudro in the final hours of planning. Together, they devised a form of sleight of hand that only the two of them could muster, the movement of the cards made by the magician, the general keeping those cards unseen by anyone else, not even his most trusted lieutenants, not even the dead.

The plan was simple on paper: three large carriers, taller than man, would be loaded into a dark assembly bay, and all men would be asked to clear it. Brooklyn would bring in his prototype through a secret entrance, completely covered to keep those who did not yet know what it was in the dark. Simultaneously, two other abandoned prototypes would be wheeled in. Inside the bay, a random carrier would be selected, and the genuine missile launcher, along with Brooklyn and his supplies, would enter it, where he would continue his work on the move. The other two carriers would be loaded with the fakes.

No one else would know which of the carriers had the real deal. Not even Rommond or Mudro. Just Brooklyn. Three platoons would be arranged to escort the carriers out into the desert, each taking a different route towards the Rift, catering for that portal's gradual movement north and south. No matter its current location, at least one group should reach it in time. Every soldier was told that their carrier contained a vital weapon, and were tasked to defend it with their lives. No one would even know there were two empty cups. It was not just a guessing game. It was a game where you did not even know you had to guess.

The three carriers, dubbed Shell, Cup, and Thimble respectively, or just A, B, and C, were each assigned a leader and a crew. Shell was marshalled by Rommond, and protected by his finest. Cup was guided by Leadman, bolstered by a fresh batch of reserves from Copperfort, along with Trokus and his band of Regime deserters. Thimble was led by Mudro, with Jacob, Whistler, and Nox making up part of its guard.

To further add to the deception, and ensure a change of plan could be made at the last minute if the real carrier came under fire, separate platoons were to be sent out into the desert, to scout ahead, to harry and distract the enemy, and to act as reinforcements along any of the three selected routes.

Rommond was not content with even this, for he handed out a dozen alternate routes for each carrier, all given in code, along with a decryption sequence (supplied by Codex Carter, who now took over from Tardo in the clock tower) that would only be used once the transports were in motion. It meant that even the drivers did not know where they were going, or how they were getting there.

It was the perfect plan. On paper. Implementing it would not be so easy.

Chapter Eleven

THE MINEFIELD MARCH

Rommond's team took the northern road, the quickest but most dangerous route, towards the last known location of the Rift, well aware that at any moment they might have to change direction to chase that elusive portal, or be chased by the enemy itself.

The journey was initially uneventful, as Rommond expected, but the general left nothing to chance, changing course periodically so that any spies that saw their advancement would be unsure of their intended destination, or the route they would take to get there. He wondered if he was being over-cautious, but the Baroness' words came back to him, urging him to come back. She never quite specified, but he thought she meant: *come back alive.*

The Shell was the most protected of all three carriers, even though Rommond himself was not certain that Brooklyn was in it, working away frantically to finish the Hometaker in time. The General had several Menacer Mark II landships, one Menacer Mark III, which he commanded directly, and a handful of smaller, more utilitarian vehicles, such as the Anchor, a larger and heavier vessel with an extra guiding wheel at the back, designed to help the carrier if it got stuck in the uneven sands; the Deafener, a larger artillery gun hauled by a half-tread truck; and the Lasher, a small landship with two arms that extended far out in front of it, clutching a rotating bar, to which were attached many long, metal chains: to clear a minefield.

This latter was brought with clear intent, for Rommond had long mapped Regime territory and made a variety of plans for theoretical incursions, few of which were tried in action. The northern path was closest to Resistance strongholds, with the fewest natural obstacles to bar the way, making it a likely line of assault for any advancing army. The Regime had spent a lot of time, money and effort on shoring up the defences along that route, the most notable being a thousand metres of mines hidden beneath the sand. Many Resistance spies had paid with their lives to find that out.

It was an odd feeling to travel across the tracks that were once the Iron Wall, and to pierce well into Regime territory, with not a bullet fired in their direction. On one hand, it was reassuring. How far they had come. On the other, it was unsettling. How far would they go?

The platoon snaked their way through the sand in single file, the mine clearer taking the lead, whipping the ground with its rotating chains, which would have set off any mines they struck, before the other landships came too close. It was a painfully slow advance, for the Lasher needed to move slowly to ensure that every strip of sand it crossed was well and truly safe. It was time well spent, but Rommond knew that they did not have much of it to spend. The Regime knew about the Hometaker. They were coming.

Then the first explosion came, and it rattled the team that had grown a little complacent by the long and quiet journey. The chains clanged and the sand swept high into the air as the first of the mines triggered. Another followed shortly after, and all the landships slowed even more, careful to ensure they stayed precisely behind the Lasher, straying not a millimetre to the left or right, where the edge of another mine could be waiting.

It was a treacherous journey, played out to the explosive percussion of the mines, which sometimes seemed to overlap one another, so that the sand barely had time to fall before it was thrown up once again. The carrier crunched over the ruined shells of the mines. If Brooklyn was inside, he would have heard those immense explosions, and was no doubt grateful that he had years prior come up with a vehicle that could disarm them.

They were halfway through, making good progress, when the mines became the least of their problems. Artillery fire started to rain down on them, tearing apart one of the Mark II landships, and setting off many of the mines in the field around.

Rommond quickly got the Deafener set up to fire its answering volley, but it was impossible to see exactly where the enemy artillery were. It seemed that they were over a large set of dunes to the north, and were playing a guessing game by firing shells into the valley below. That was good for the carrier, because the targeting was random, but bad for the Deafener, because it too had to make shots in the dark.

So the rounds were fired, back and forth, like a game of badminton over a net of sand, a game where you did not want to catch the shuttlecock. The Deafener held back away from the carrier, so as not to inadvertently draw the enemy's attention towards it. They could afford for the artillery gun to be destroyed, not the carrier.

Throughout this back and forth of ear-rending gunfire, the mine clearer continued its careful advancement, followed eagerly by the carrier. Yet each explosion in the minefield now presented a new danger: the risk of highlighting just where their advancement was. Volleys started to rain down closer to the carrier, while others continued to aim for the artillery gun. The enemy had many at its disposal, so it did not have to be picky.

"Keep up the pace," Rommond urged. Then he directed the drivers of the other landships to follow him. He broke rank, letting the artillery gun continue to boom, and the carrier advance, while he guided the rest of the platoon back from where they had come, and around the edge of the gigantic dune. There, they spotted a row of three artillery guns, a little smaller than the Deafener, but just as deadly.

The artillery loaders were caught off guard, so much so that one set loaded a shell wrongly, resulting in the entire gun exploding in their faces. The other two guns went down to turret fire from Rommond's landships, and the fleeing gunners did not flee for long.

Yet this small victory came with the revelation of defeat, for from this vantage point they saw, through the smoke and fire of the ruined artillery, a black strip on the horizon, which Rommond's seasoned eyes knew was a massive army advancing their way.

Chapter Twelve

PUSH ON

"Quick!" Rommond cried when he returned to the carrier. "We've got to clear the path ahead."

"We're already clearing it," Lieutenant Algrip replied. He was standing waist-high from the hatch on the mine clearer, relaying to the team inside the general's need of haste.

"We need to clear it faster," Rommond said, firing several bullets from his revolver into the sand ahead. One of them bounced off a hidden mine, sending the sand sky-high once more.

The others joined him in this new-found technique, unloading magazines and barrels into the deceptively empty sand around. The general gave them sections to concentrate on, which would result in a zig-zagging path for the carrier to go through.

"Why not straight?" he was asked.

"Because an army is on our tail, and we want to clear the way for us, not for them."

So they cleared by gunfire as well as by the spinning chains of the Lasher, which pressed forward a little faster than the engineers recommended. There was little time for caution now. The enemy was hot on their trail.

"We're spending a lot of ammunition on this," Algrip warned. He was always rather frugal in battle, Rommond noticed, which at any other time he would have commended.

"If we don't get out of here quick, we won't be able to spend those bullets any other way," he growled. "If we saved every single shot we had, we still wouldn't have enough for the army that's coming."

"So we're fleeing?"

"You damn well bet we are! We're fighting this on *our* terms, not theirs."

If the enemy had not known their location by now, they would have seen the leaping sand from a great distance away, and the regular ringing of metal as mine shells joined the jumping grains.

I kind of hope you're not in there, Brooklyn, Rommond thought to himself, caressing the side of the carrier. *I hope you went on the easier paths*. He had to stop himself there. There were no easier paths now. It was all an uphill struggle to topple the king at the top.

A passage was cleared for more than three quarters of the way, but there was still room to go. And yet, the enemy started to appear on the dune overhead, where the waiting Deafener took its first carefully-aimed shots. The first of those Regime landships, square and solid, fell to those shells, but more came through the haze of sand, smoke, and fire. Some aimed at the artillery gun, but many more aimed at the bulky carrier, whose size made it a noticeable—and easy—target.

"Push on!" Rommond cried, diving into the

driving seat of his landship, while his gunner rotated the turret into place. The enemy had the higher ground, but the general had the greater experience, and the greater speed. His vessel evaded the rounds of the enemy, but many were not even firing at him.

If Brooklyn was inside that carrier, spanner and screwdriver in hand, he would have trembled at the rattle of gunfire off the reinforced hull. Though none of the bullets pierced it yet, they were leaving larger and larger dents in the surface. If a single shot got through and struck the engineer inside, it could end all of their hopes of reclaiming their home and putting an end to this war.

So, even as Rommond tried to draw the enemy fire, and his gunner took down some of the landships overhead, a few of the Resistance fighters continued to hand-pick empty spots in the desert to clear the minefield, and the Lasher continued to pick up the pace, against all advice to the contrary.

Push on! was the motto of the day, even as the day was quickly waning, and the sun threatened to throw darkness into the mix, where all would be wary, unsure if they might tread upon sand or metal, or the feet of the enemy, or into the cross-hairs of their guns.

Then, as the carrier came to the last of the known section of the minefield, the Lasher's haste was their undoing. The metal chains continued their frantic whipping of the sand, but the acceleration was faster than the spinning, so that whole strips of sand went unwhipped. The treads of the vehicle pressed down upon the pressure plate of an unexploded mine, tearing the mine clearer apart, and sending its chains out in all directions, where some exploded other mines, and some struck the hulls of other vehicles, even lashing at Rommond's own landship.

It also had another effect.

The explosion was so great, enhanced by the fuel and fire of the mine clearer's engines, that the carrier that followed swiftly and closely behind, was rocked by the force, and knocked over onto its side. The explosion cast a great wind out around it, which cleared many of the grains in all directions, exposing a handful of other unexploded devices that were now dangerously close to the carrier. They had gotten to the edge of safety, but it was just the edge, where you were not safe enough.

Chapter Thirteen

THE MEDICAL CONVOY

Back in Blackout, those left behind were growing restless. The Hometaker project had helped motivate people, and gave many a job to do. Some of those now left without work donned a uniform, joining the Resistance ranks. Others were left to fade away in the foggy streets of the city.

One of the restless was Lorelai. She had watched the landships roll out, and waved to the men, like so many other women waved, and threw a white rose out to them, like all those wives and mothers and sisters did. White roses, not red. A symbol of peace, not war.

Then the vehicles vanished into the dunes, with the only identifying mark being the cloud of smoke that wafted with them. To many eyes, it seemed like another smog-smothered city crawling across the desert plains.

The women went back to work, if they had jobs, or back to their families, if they had families. There were human women and maran women, and mostly maran children, though everyone looked largely the same. There were a handful of human babies, one born from one of the Pure, and the others born in recent days, after Taberah's successful destruction of the Birth-masters. Things were changing, and that feeling of change and hope filled the air. It passed from eye to eye, and mouth to ear. You could see it and feel it and taste it, and it made many people happy, overcoming their anxiousness about their loved ones who once again marched to war. It did not make Lorelai happy. It made her more anxious than ever. Things were changing. She feared they were changing for the worse.

She was inadvertently ushered away with a group of women after the men departed and brought into someone's home, one still marked with gunfire from Rommond's trip through the city in the Hopebreaker all those weeks ago. She tried to say she had things to do, and she did, but her training kicked in like instincts, and told her to try to blend in. The other women went, so she went. It was precisely why she was there when the landships left in the first place, why she was holding a white rose, when she knew she was sworn to red.

"My Tom'll have 'em sorted," one Geraldine, an older women, said. She wore a faded floral-pattern dress, a little big for her, with not much shape to it. Lorelai felt herself document the details, like she had done so many times before on her scouting trips. It was the details that mattered when you had to blend in, when you had to immerse yourself in a foreign culture and change the population without anyone there even knowing it.

"My money's on Rommond," one Carol replied. It was her home (after it was taken from someone else), and she was pouring the tea into a row of porcelain cups. She was maran. Lorelai could sense it, but Carol's loyalties clearly lay with the Resistance. She had that air about her, that air of defiance.

"You haven't got any money," Geraldine replied.

The women laughed, so Lorelai laughed.

"I know what you mean though," one Urla said. She was the youngest of the lot, a brunette, barely in her prime. Her husband had just recently been promoted by the general. They were both honoured. Lorelai knew better. She had tried to sew up many of Rommond's "promotions" before.

"If anyone can do it," Geraldine said, "it'll be Ricochet Rommond."

"What about you, dear?" Carol asked, addressing Lorelai now. "Got a man on the front line?"

Lorelai blushed. She had learned to blush when blushing was called for, but she felt it was a little more real this time. "Yes," she said shyly. She did not need to be shy, but here it helped. "We're not together very long."

"And he's whisked away already," Carol replied. "I think they do it deliberately. Leave us at home with the kids!"

"I kind of wonder though," Lorelai said, "if I should be out there. It doesn't feel right to be stuck here. I'm a field nurse. I should be out there, helping them, healing them."

"We've got plenty to heal here," Geraldine commented. "The infirmary's packed with 'em!"

"I know, but having first aid out there on the field can make a huge difference. It could help win the war. I mean, what if Rommond was hurt? What if we needed someone to get to him quick?"

Urla spoke into her cup her common refrain: "I know what you mean."

Lorelai wondered what she would do if she found the general out there, if it was up to her to save him. She thought she might, but if Rommond would topple the Iron Emperor, then he was a threat to her people. Maybe she would let him bleed.

"So, why aren't you out there then?" Carol asked.

"Don't be daft!" Geraldine interjected. "She probably has the kids to mind."

"No kids," Lorelai replied.

"You're lucky," Geraldine said with a chuckle. "I had ten. Most of 'em were before the Harvest though. And you know what, I don't care what people say about 'em, whether they're 'demons' or not. They're my flesh and blood, so they are. I raised 'em and reared 'em, and they cried the same, and slept the same, and soiled the same, bless 'em!"

Carol laughed. "Sure yours are as good as twins."

"I *had* twins afore that time, and they're more different than the two I had after, barely a year apart. That boy and girl are the image of each other."

"And the image of you!" Carol said. "But here, Lorelai, is it? Why don't you go out then if you feel it's what you should be doing?"

"I don't know," Lorelai said. "Duty, I guess."

"Duty to who?"

Of course, Lorelai could not say she was following orders, that she had been assigned to Blackout by the Pilgrimage, the scouting wing of the Iron Empire.

That was her duty, and yet she thought maybe she could fulfil it better in a different way, by getting out there, by joining the fight.

"The city," Lorelai said eventually.

Carol scoffed. "What has this city ever done for you, eh? Since this war started, it's been in everyone's hands, like a black marble lost and won by every kid around. It's no one's *home* now, love. The only reason no one's really noticed is because of that cloud of smog that's gotten worse since the war started, and that smog in people's heads that makes them look the other way. You don't owe this city any more than you owe the Treasury, and, by God, I think they owe us, the thieving sods."

Lorelai dwelt on this for a moment, like she dwelt on so much else. "I guess you're right."

The night deepened before Lorelai could escape her captors and return to the infirmary, where she had helped Whistler forget his troubles by focusing on the troubles of others. He patched some people up, and seemed to enjoy the work. She remembered Jacob standing in the doorway watching them and smiling. She hated what he might think of her now. *You wouldn't understand*, she thought.

Urla went with her. She had not realised that she was a nurse too. She spent so much time focusing on the wounds that her fellow nurses went unnoticed. It was a failing as a scout too. She knew she cared too much. It was hard to work in a job of healing and not start to care about the people you healed.

She managed to convince some of the other

nurses to join her. Urla took no convincing at all. She knew she was using them as cover. It looked less suspicious if she was part of a convoy. So they loaded up their supplies into three half-track trucks, brightly emblazoned with a white cross. They were old vehicles, scratched and weathered, with engines that groaned noisily, and parts that creaked and squeaked as it moved. And they rolled out, like the landships before, only there was no one in the streets to wish them farewell, and no white roses to pray for peace.

Some of the other nurses were optimistic. They were city nurses. They saw horror, but did not see the horrors of the battlefield. While many bodies went back, battered and broken, the worst never went back at all. They had to deal with the aftermath. They did not see the battle, the bloodshed, the hatred. They did not see those caught by the flamethrowers, or those who burned inside from the mustard gas. Some called her home world Hell, but she saw Hell here too. She walked those red sands.

"Can't wait to do my part," Urla said. She clutched her box of supplies close to her chest, like a newborn. She had mentioned she wanted a child. Now she could have a human one, if both her and her husband survived. It was unlikely.

"Here's to saving people," one of the other nurses said cheerfully.

Lorelai forced a smile, and joined in their toast. She never said what she thought. *Here's to saving mine.*

Chapter Fourteen

SANDSTONE BRIDGE

"Hell," Jacob said as he tried to sort through the various maps. "Rommond doesn't make this easy."

"Good," Nox said. "We don't want it easy."

Jacob shrugged. "I wouldn't mind."

He rummaged through several more maps, before passing them to Whistler. "Find me 5A. That's where the codes suggest we go next."

They were not given much time to pack. No one was. Supplies were haphazardly thrown into the trucks and landships, and the troops were thrown in too.

Whistler found the right map and proudly handed it to Jacob. The Coilhunter grabbed the edge of it and stared at the features with his dark, cold eyes.

"Sandstone Bridge," he mused ominously.

Mudro sighed.

"Is that a bad thing?" Jacob asked.

"I don't know," Nox said. "We ain't got there yet. But it's the perfect place to lay a trap."

"Well, maybe we *do* want it easy then, eh?"

"We want a straight fight. No tricks."

"Coming from you."

Nox eyed him coldly. "What's that supposed to mean?"

"Eh, well … all your gadgets."

"You mean the unfettered fingers of the law?"

Jacob raised an eyebrow. "I mean the butterflies and ducks."

Nox grumbled.

"So, what do we do when we get to the bridge?" Whistler intervened.

"We cross it," Nox said. "Hopefully."

They arrived at Sandstone Bridge around an hour later, spotting its vast arch and many pillars from a distance. It looked like an ancient construct, something that belonged in the Dune Burrows, and whatever river it might have crossed in its prime had long dried up.

"We shouldn't overload the bridge, just in case," Jacob suggested. He strolled with Whistler alongside the carrier. The cockpit was too hot and too cramped. Even Mudro sat on top, leaving the driver inside alone.

"This stone would hold a Behemoth," Mudro replied. "I don't think we have to worry about that."

The carrier rolled out slowly onto the bridge. The columns supporting the immense stone structure creaked beneath its weight, and its own hull creaked to match. It was a dreadfully slow advance, thanks to all that it carried, and its plodding pace filled everyone there with dread.

"It's a long stretch to go," Nox said, rolling along beside it in his monowheel. He peered across the bridge at the many columns on either side, behind which he could not see.

"This is apparently the safest road," Mudro commented. "Rommond gave himself the hardest path. But his is the quickest route, less winding. Ours will have us late to the party."

"I don't mind late," Jacob said. "Just as long as we arrive."

There was the sound of tumbling scree. A tiny plume of dust rose on the other side of the bridge, near one of the gigantic pillars. All eyes fixed on it, but it seemed like nothing more than the shifting of · the earth.

"Can't we get this moving any faster?" Jacob urged. "I feel *exposed* out here."

"Not unless we empty the carrier," Mudro replied, "and we're not doing that."

Nox stopped suddenly, and ushered the others to halt as well. It took a moment for the carrier to grind to a halt. Mudro swayed on top.

Nox placed his boot down on the ground beside his monowheel, leaning the vehicle that way. He rubbed the heel, until it exposed a black wire beneath the dust.

"It's a trap!" he cried.

Before any of them could turn, a series of explosions rocked the bridge. The wires connected to sticks of dynamite strapped to a number of the columns supporting the arch. Many of them ignited, sending rock and sand sky high, and the support structure tumbling down.

In the panic and the rocking and the storm of

sand that followed, no one knew what to do, or where to go. It was not clear if the front or the back of the bridge was collapsing, and so whether to press ahead or make a quick retreat. They were not even sure which way was which, but for the carrier planted in the middle of them all, steady and unmoving.

When the haze settled just a little, it was clear that the way behind them no longer existed. There was a giant, jagged precipice only metres away from their feet, and not far from the carrier's treads. The middle and front of the bridge were still intact—for now.

Yet, even as the company let out their first sighs of relief, the stone beneath them shifted slightly.

"Eh," Jacob blurted. "This isn't looking good."

"We have to get off this bridge," Mudro said, slapping his hand down on the carrier's hull. The driver started it up again, adding its own smoke to the haze. It pushed forward just a little, and the ground moaned audibly beneath. Then another tremor came, bigger than the last. Larger rocks catapulted down from the pillars overhead and the columns beneath, crashing apart where they fell, each adding its own small part to the upheaval.

The carrier halted, chugging to a stop.

"If we move," Mudro said, glancing down, "we might set off a chain reaction."

"If we don't move," Jacob replied, glancing up, "it might go off anyway."

The answer to the question came from somewhere else. Further ahead, behind the few solid pillars left standing, came the rattle of well-aimed gunfire. Mudro yelped as one struck his arm, and many of the company dived behind the carrier, which took the brunt of the bullets.

"Aren't we supposed to be defending this thing?" Jacob shouted over the metal pings.

They heard the revving of an engine, and saw the thick black smoke that bellowed from the Coilhunter's monowheel like a veil. That was answer enough.

Nox sped across the stone platform, ignoring the shaking, ducking from gunfire, and dodging falling stones. He saw snipers peeping out from behind the pillars. He advanced on them, whipping out his pistol as he drove, launching a few perfect shots at the heads of his attackers.

Yet they were many, and just as he was aiming for another sniper at the right, several more fired at him from the left. One struck his gun, knocking it from his hand. Before he had time to unearth another, he felt the monowheel go over a now familiar bump: black wire.

This explosion was more deafening than the first, because it was closer than before. He kept driving, feeling a hail of stone from the snipers of the gods, seeing little in the miasma of smoke and dust.

Then he felt a sudden drop, the kind that took the core of him and sent it into his throat. He could barely see anything, but he knew he was falling, that the monowheel was falling. It was heavy, so it fell quick, and it dragged him down with it.

He plummeted so fast that for a brief moment he came out of the explosive haze, able to briefly see the crumbling hole in the bridge above him, and the still-falling blocks from the pillar around him.

He seized a handle on the right side of the control panel, which released a giant grappling hook from the front right of the monowheel. It wrapped around one of the still-standing columns that the Regime shooters hid behind, tugging tight, almost reefing the metal from the monowheel as it stopped its descent.

Then it swung, like a giant pendulum, towards the pillar that saved it. Yet it also struck the cliff-face ahead, its metal tracks dragging across the granite, until the drag sent the wheel spinning as it swung, making it impossible for Nox to find the perfect aim to fire the other grappling hook on the other side.

He lurched back into the falling cloud of dust and debris, came out briefly on the other side, then careened back down again, through the thick blackness, before his pendulum vessel arrived almost back where it started. From there, still spinning, and slowing just a moment before beginning its downward pivot, Nox took the best aim he could, and said a silent prayer. He fired the left grappling hook, and it took hold around one of the other pillars on the other side.

The monowheel stabilised, but the force of the sudden grasp sent Nox flailing from his seat. He grabbed at anything, only to pull hard on the lever that put the vehicle into automatic acceleration, before he fell a foot or two and grabbed a hold of the metal basket at the back, his two feet dangling overboard. The treads around the wheel span like crazy, eroding the rock. Nox felt himself falling further. His feet swung into the path of the spinning tracks, grinding through the leather. He cried out and tried to pull away, then jolted as a piece of the metal he gripped came apart in his hand.

This isn't it, he thought to himself. *This isn't how you die.* He always thought that it would be the Wild North that would kill him. *Not out here. Not while there's still bounties to cash.*

He gave it his all, hauling himself back up into the driver's seat, which now faced up towards the sky. He plopped his back against the leather, turned off the automatic, and pressed his bruised boot against the accelerator.

The monowheel's tracks gripped the uneven outcroppings of the cliff-face, grinding them into dust, but it propelled it upwards, even as Nox tightened the wire on the grappling hooks. Together, with the pushing of the wheel and the pulling of the ropes, the monowheel ascended the wall beneath the bridge, and clambered over the ravine to the other side.

Nox let loose the grappling wire and dived from his seat, even as the snipers turned in shock to him. He tumbled in the sand, casting three tiny canisters behind him, and casting two bullets from his second pistol ahead. The canisters exploded after a few seconds, sending out a hail of smaller canisters attached to magnets. Many of these flew straight for the guns of the bewildered snipers at the rear, only to release a blinding flash of light as they struck home. The snipers ahead were not used to close-quarters fighting. They were already dead. It was not long before the rest of them joined them, and Nox "acquired" one of their pistols to replace his own.

The Coilhunter caught his breath, and let out another plume of smoke from his mask. He barely had time for a second gasp, however, when he saw a large crack worming through the bridge towards the carrier.

Chapter Fifteen

THE EDGE

At Sandstone Bridge, the ground shifted again, this time more violently than before. The team upon the bridge wavered in place as large cracks crept through the rock towards them.

"We've got to make a run for it," Jacob urged, pulling Whistler by the sleeve.

"What about the carrier?" Whistler asked, resting his hand on it for support.

"There's no time."

"Go," Mudro told them. "There's nothing you can do here."

"What about you?" Whistler asked.

Another tremor, and the cracks became crevices.

"Go!" Mudro shouted.

Jacob pulled Whistler on, until both were running. Their speed was slowed by the uneven earth and the many obstacles that appeared out of nowhere just ahead of them. They leapt over ever-growing chasms, rolled out of the way of falling boulders, clambered over broken pillars, and covered their faces with their arms as clouds of dust exploded in front of them.

They saw Nox far ahead on the other side, dealing

his last blows, then turning to them, eyes wide with horror, and then dashing towards them, feet whipped by haste.

Yet, even as they raced, the ground gave way more and more beneath and around them. Just as they reached halfway, the giant slab of rock they ran across dropped suddenly. One of the supporting pillars on the left gave way, and the slab tilted down in that direction, till it caught the crumbling column and clung precariously to its tip.

The slope was so great now that neither Jacob nor Whistler could race across. They fell, and skidded down the stone slide, Whistler on his back, Jacob spinning on his chest, the gravel tearing through his shirt and grazing his ribs. Whistler was closest to the edge, and so he would have been the first to plummet off, were it not for Jacob's extra weight, and his headlong dive towards the boy, arms outstretched, as if somehow he could save him, and not just dive off to their death together.

He reached one skint hand towards the boy, and Whistler tried to reach back, stretching his head back to see. His vision was taken by the vast sky above, and the clear, sharp edge of the slope below, growing closer to his feet by the second.

Then finally Jacob grabbed the boy's hand, and even in the tumult and the tumble he could see the brief relief in Whistler's face. He wished he could have shown his own, but now he had to stop them from falling over the edge. He stretched out his other hand, everywhere and anywhere, his fingers desperately feeling for some nook or ledge, some small outcropping or indentation that he could grab a hold of. All he could feel was sand and scree. Whenever he thought he caught hold of something solid, it came away from the slab and fell down with him. The rocks fell and the dust fell, and if you listened really closely, you could hear their tiny, stony screams.

The edge came.

Jacob felt Whistler's grip tightening, and his own instinctively tightened too. They were holding onto nothing, just each other. They could not even hold onto hope. The edge consumed that too.

Then the slab shook violently once more, and they felt a sudden drop. For a moment, Jacob thought they had slipped over the ravine. Then he found the slab tilting up, and he realised that a column on the far side had given way. The slide shifted. It was now more of a see-saw, and while Jacob started to skid down the other way, Whistler fell, feet over head, until Jacob's firm grip brought him upright.

And they slid again, back from where they had come, back with their comrades the dust and debris, back past the sparsity of grips and hooks and footfalls, back towards the drop on the other side. No matter where they fell, the edge was always there to greet them.

And it came all the faster, for the slope was steeper than before. This time even Whistler flailed his other arm about for something else to grip, even though there was no chance he could support both his and Jacob's weight.

Fair play for trying, Jacob thought, when he had a moment from his own flailing to think.

And suddenly the smuggler caught something with his reaching fingers. A little shard of stone from one of the fallen pillars was still embedded into its base, firm as any foundation, unless the bridge decided to quake again. He gripped it tight and felt his muscles tear and spasm as he caught the whole of his weight as well as Whistler's. As his fingers strained, he was glad his grip was strong, and glad the boy was light.

He held on for dear life, for life was very dear, and Whistler held on tight to him. Yet it was a precarious hold, and they were both at the mercy of the see-saw of the gods. If it turned on them again, Jacob knew he would lose his grip, and they would be back sliding down to where there were none. Then the ever-patient edge would have its prize, and the war would be lost or won by others.

So he prayed for stability, for no shifting, for no rock to rub against another rock, no stone to shove another stone. He prayed for the pillars to hold, both the ones beneath, which were stopped mid-fall by the ceiling that came down on them, and the ones still standing on the unbroken part of the bridge, which still shuddered and cracked as Mudro carefully led the carrier across it.

From this vantage point, many feet below the main bridge, Jacob could see Nox appearing at the cliff, peering down with his worried eyes, his hands working frantically to load up a reclaimed grappling hook to one of the pressurised shooters at the front of his monowheel.

"You okay down there?" Jacob shouted to

Whistler, whose grip seemed to be weakening. The smuggler tightened his own to compensate, but the strain was getting to him too.

"No," Whistler replied, his dust-filled hair ravaged by the breeze. He squinted as he looked up, and even though his eyes were half-closed, Jacob could see the fear in them. The sun reached down to them as well, not to haul them up, but to offer them a scalding hand, to drain the last of their already waning strength, and poke them in the eye with its many blinding rays. The sun was a friend of no one, but today it was a friend of the edge.

"Hey, you're the one who likes heights," Jacob called down. Even up there, dangling, he thought he could lighten the mood.

Whistler replied with a grimace. He liked to fly, not to fall.

On the remainder of the bridge, Mudro eased the carrier across at a snail's pace. It was no longer a straight run. There were holes and dips everywhere, forcing him to zig-zag around. That made it worse, because the carrier was big and clunky, and did not turn well. Every manoeuvre had to be carefully orchestrated, every pivot planned, every zig with a plea, every zag with a prayer.

The ground continued to quake momentarily, threatening to send the carrier down like Jacob and Whistler. Mudro had to put them out of his mind, even though he could see them dangling out of the corner of his eye. He had to speak Rommond's words to himself: *Stick to the mission. Men can fall. The plan only falls if men dive.*

He saw Nox far ahead, working on his vehicle, stuffing the cable back into its holster. There was a huge gap between them, bridged only by a short, winding path. How Mudro wished then that he could do more than conjure cards or orchestrate illusions. In another world, in Iraldas, he could have made a phantom crossing. But in that same world, the snipers would not have been shooting at him with lead. No, this was a world of iron and sand, of physical things, where death did not send you to the afterlife to influence the living from afar, but finished you off for good. The game of life was different here, and you had to play by its rules.

The treads of the carrier crunched against the cracked earth, and Mudro walked along beside it, patting it periodically to help guide the driver in the well-sealed cockpit at the front. For a moment, he wondered if Brooklyn was in the back, hearing those raps and taps, making his own muffled sounds inside, and urging them to rescue him, to save his world-claiming creation at all costs. He put the thought out of his mind. Rommond wanted them to treat all three carriers as equal, until the moment when Brooklyn himself, and only him, would make the big reveal. Mudro just hoped that if he died for this one, he would not have died in vain.

Then the earth cracked ahead of them. It was a thin crack, but it was growing, and it was right in the trajectory of the carrier. The choice was not a choice. They could either steam ahead, as the ground gave way, or wait for whatever island they were on to fall like the rest into the rocky rapids below.

Mudro banged hard on the side of the carrier, as if the driver needed any extra encouragement. The doctor stayed on foot, so as not to add any extra weight to the carrier, and trotted alongside it as it picked up steam.

From there—slowed by his limp, but hastened by his fear—he saw that Nox was preparing to fire his newly-reloaded grappling hook down to Jacob and Whistler. Yet, on seeing the creeping crack in the path of the carrier, Jacob's faint shout ushered the Coilhunter to save the vehicle instead. In that moment, as Nox reluctantly fired the hook towards the carrier, Mudro hoped that if Jacob and Whistler died for this one, they too would not have died in vain.

The hook grappled into place around one of the handles on the outside of the carrier, but just like those two dangling people down below, it was a precarious grip. It hung by just one of its three curved nails. Mudro, mid-run, tried to adjust it, but the tether was tight. Even as the carrier sailed across the ever-growing gap, the wire pulled tighter. It was better than nothing, but Mudro feared it might not be enough.

On the other side, Nox drove his monowheel around one of the two remaining pillars, wrapping the wire around, before heading towards the second. With two in place, it might just be enough to support the weight of the carrier, even if it was hanging by a nail.

But he never made it to the second column. The

chasm widened, and the mountainous maw conspired with gravity and yanked the carrier down into its gape. The wire pulled tighter, and the monowheel sped backwards towards the first pillar, crushing against the stone. Nox kept the acceleration on, but there just was not enough weight, power or grip to do anything but linger.

The carrier fell down onto a huge stone slab just like the one that Jacob and Whistler clung to, only this one did not tilt to the side; it tilted back and up, leading like a ramp to the other side of the bridge. Mudro hung out of the side, his own nails digging into one of the handles. It was a stroke of luck in a multitude of misfortunes, but it felt like only a momentary reprieve, for safety taunted them from above, and gravity still beckoned from below.

The grappling hook held for now, but the angry sounds of the monowheel up above, and the straining of that metal nail around the handle, suggested it would not hold for long. The driver pressed hard on the pedal, and the tracks ground against the earth, kicking away the slippery sand, gripping the road as if even iron did not want to fall.

Then the wire snapped, and all seemed lost. Were it not for the less steep slope, the carrier would have plummeted immediately. Instead, it started to slide back down, losing all the ground it had made, like a symbol of the back and forth of war, before the ultimate oblivion.

The driver threw everything he had into acceleration, switching gears, shovelling coal with one hand, yanking levers with the other. Both feet he kept down on the accelerators, and both treads span around the hull, fighting gravel and gravity, not moving forward, but not moving backwards either.

And then the treads seemed to give way a little, and the carrier slipped down, before the tracks caught on a more uneven patch of rock, stopping it again. Yet, even as it halted, the spinning tracks were like a grindstone, wearing down the little outcroppings that kept the vehicle from slipping away entirely. When it advanced, it ascended inches, but when it fell back, it slipped by feet. There was only so long that battle of measurements could last.

To the side of the carrier, Mudro hung, contemplating for a moment the possibility of letting go, and so freeing the carrier of the burden of his weight.

Down below to the left, Jacob and Whistler could do nothing but wait and watch, and cling and clutch, and hope. Up above, Nox worked furiously to dislodge the second grappling hook from the second pillar and load it back into the pressurised cannon on his monowheel.

In time, he succeeded, and fired the hook back down to the carrier, where Mudro helped guide its grip into place. The Coilhunter had already secured the rope around the second pillar. Then he fired up his monowheel and tried to haul the carrier up. Now it ascended not just by inches, cruising up the slope even as the monowheel span like crazy, and the wire dug deep into the pillar's frame.

Then, just as the carrier neared the top, just enough for even Mudro to reach his hand out to the ledge, the supporting wire around the pillar bit too deep. The column rocked. It seemed like just at the moment of salvation, safety was snatched from them.

Nox and the carrier's driver kept pushing metal, and the wire kept slicing stone. Just as the pillar looked like it might snap, the carrier clambered over the edge, back onto solid ground. Mudro collapsed to the earth, and Nox stopped the monowheel, breathing a smokey sigh of relief.

They were safe. The carrier was safe.

Yet the pillar still rocked, and even before their first breath was caught, the top half, where the wire dug deep, snapped apart and collapsed down into the ravine, to where Jacob and Whistler were still holding on. The column struck the top of the slab they were on, then began to roll side-long like a boulder towards them. If they hung on, it would crush them. If they let go, they would fall down to their doom.

The horror of it all washed over everyone.

Up above, Jacob saw the rolling column coming down fast. Down below, he saw Whistler's horrified expression.

"Sorry, kid," he said.

Sorry it had to end this way.

Then he let go.

Chapter Sixteen

HAMMERFALL ON
THE HOME FRONT

In Blackout, the city was quiet. Rommond's curfew was still in operation, helping to stabilise the previous unrest from the many changeovers. The streets were empty, with no footsteps penetrating through the grey smoke. As the night wore on, the smoke of the chimneys fizzled out, and the lights in the windows faded with them.

Guards were still on duty, switching shifts, but there were few left. Many had gone with the armies into the east. That was where the battle was. Those who remained nodded off at their posts, and even the most vigilant among them grew weary, until their watch was no longer truly kept.

Royce left the butchers at close to midnight. He always did longer days than most. He hung up his apron and locked up, making sure to only take a small amount of coils with him. He had made that mistake before, and paid for it with the loss of a week's income, and almost paid for it with his life.

He leant against his walking stick and glanced up at the moon before he stepped down off the porch step. It was particularly bright tonight, or maybe the city was just particularly dark. He decided against the use of a lantern. He knew he should not be out this late. The general was not there, but he insisted that his curfew was kept, and his guards passed on that insistence to the locals very clearly.

He hobbled through the smog, slowly at first, then a little more hurriedly when he thought he heard a sound behind him. He stopped, just in time to catch what he thought was a boot scraping through the gravel, and shuffled off even faster than before. He clutched the handle of his walking stick more tightly, and wondered if it would be enough in a fight.

He felt his heart hammer against the anvil of his chest, and the ice of the night made his breathing difficult and more painful than normal. He started to trot, driving the walking stick into the ground before him, diving through the fog with just his instinct and intuition, and the pale glimmer of moonlight, to guide him.

The boots continued to kill the gravel behind him, but it was a long, slow stride, compared to Royce's short, frantic one. It was someone calm and collected, with a form of military march. It was the kind of thing you expected if you broke Rommond's curfew, because if you did, you expected to meet him out there in the streets.

Royce continued on as fast as his knackered legs could propel him, until he turned a corner and saw a light on in the bakery, with the worn sign reading Daily Dough. That was Erswell's store. He set up shop not long after Royce himself. He was someone you could count on, someone you could trust.

Royce banged on the door with one hand, leaning heavily with the other on his support. He cast a worried eye back into the smog behind him, still hearing the faint echo of footsteps. He blasted the panels of the door again, until Erswell opened it slowly, bemused.

"What's all this racket, Royce?"

"I thought I heard someone."

"So did I," Erswell said, "banging at my door at this unholy hour."

"No," Royce said earnestly, stressing the word. "Someone … military."

Erswell's eyes lit up, and he ushered Royce inside. Before Royce had even closed the door behind him, making sure to seal all the latches, the younger man buried his head in an open chest nearby, rummaging through the belongings inside.

"You didn't really prepare for this, did you?" Royce asked.

"I prepared enough," the baker replied, pulling out a rifle.

"Do you even remember how to shoot it?"

Erswell cocked his head. Then he cocked the gun.

The duo returned to the streets, walking stick and rifle in hand. The footsteps had faded, leaving only their own nervous footfalls to echo through the alleys. They tried to walk slowly, to mask their movements, but they knew that time was against them. They had to hurry.

The butcher's and bakery were both in the same quarter of the city, along with other produce providers. They served civilians most of the time, but they also served the guard post at the southern gate, and a military porter distributed food from there to the other posts. It meant they knew the main guard, Trem, quite well. He was likely to be on duty that night. Someone they could count on. Someone they could trust.

They continued through, painfully aware of the openness of the main road they were traversing, with only the cover of the smog to hide them. It sprung to both of their minds that the back alleys were a sneakier route, but that made it sneakier for other people too. Depending on who ran the city, those laneways were populated by crooks and thieves, some solo and others in a guild, and there were unwritten agreements in place with the guards to look the other way. Though Rommond had put a stop to much of that, some of the guilds had just gone into hiding. Now that he was away once more, it was the perfect time for them to return to the darkest alleys. It meant it was safer to travel in the open streets, where the guards still had full jurisdiction.

Yet neither Royce nor Erswell felt safe. As much as they had witnessed the war come to their doorsteps, and swore allegiance to the Resistance, then to the Treasury, and now to the Resistance again, they were not used to the stress and strain of being out in it all. They had watched. They watched from the windows. Watched from behind their counters. Watching was easy.

The marching beat of the boots returned behind them, and they rushed forward, creating a frenzied patter between each rhythmic thud. It was clear from the pace that it was not someone chasing them, but the sound chased their ears all the same.

They saw the guard post rising out of the fog up ahead, illuminated by a dim gaslight, which gave the wisps of smoke a ghostly air. The appearance of a sanctuary spurred them on even more.

Royce banged on the door of the hut just like he had done at Erswell's bakery. It took longer for Trem to answer, and when he did he was wiping the sleep from his eyes.

"Royce," he exclaimed. "Erswell. What are you two doing here?"

"We heard someone," Royce replied, pushing himself inside.

"What's that?" Trem said with a yawn.

"Someone *military*."

The word brought alertness to Trem's eyes like cold water. He pulled Erswell into the hut and sealed the door behind them, before grabbing his rifle from the wall. He pushed the barrel through a slit in the panels, and peered out into the gloom.

"How close?" he asked.

"Very," Erswell said.

"Right on our tail!" Royce added.

Then they hushed, for the sound of the boots grew close. All three of them looked out, waiting for the figure to appear. They were half-eager and half-fearful. The footsteps were getting louder now, but still the smog shielded the man inside.

And then he appeared: a tall man in Regime uniform, carrying a pistol in his hand.

"My God," Trem whispered. "How did *he* get in here?"

Royce looked to Erswell with worried eyes.

"There's probably more of them," the guard continued.

"What will we do?" Royce pleaded, clutching his walking stick tightly.

"We need to issue an alert."

"How?" Erswell asked. "We don't have radios here."

"Rommond has plenty in the old clock tower."

Erswell glanced at Royce, but Royce's attention was fixed on the Regime soldier outside. To Royce's eyes, which were pretty good despite his age, that soldier looked a lot like Hamhart, the innkeeper of *The Horse and Hook*. The gaslight was faint, but it shone just enough that Royce could make out the recognisable bristles joining the man's sideburns to his chin.

"I've got a shot," Trem said, carefully aiming his rifle. "I can take him out."

Trem was always a good shot. He usually only needed one. But Royce was good as well. As Trem's finger hovered over the trigger, Royce's hovered over the handle of his walking stick. In a fraction of a second, he pulled the handle, unleashing a blade from the top. In the next fraction, as Trem's finger rubbed the trigger, Royce stabbed the guard in the back. He only needed one stab.

Trem fell, collapsing onto his rifle. Erswell opened the door of the hut and waved to Hamhart. The innkeeper gave the Regime salute, which Erswell gave in kind. Hamhart strolled up to the entrance of the hut, glancing down at Trem bleeding out slowly on the floor. It seemed like the guard was trying to whisper something, perhaps a curse, perhaps a plea for help. It was not even clear that he knew what had happened.

"Nasty business," Royce said, wiping the blood off the blade, before sheathing it back in his walking stick. "Kind of thing you'd want an apron for." He arched his back for a good stretch, then hunched over again so as not to break character for too long. The disguise had to become a habit, or you got in the bad habit of dropping the disguise.

"Nasty, yes," Hamhart said, "but someone's got to do it." He smiled, like he did when serving drinks, as if he thought that "someone" should be him. "We have the north and west gates. The east should come in soon."

"You're not exactly going for *subtle*, are you?" Erswell said, gesturing to the innkeeper's uniform. It looked brand new, with the folds still crisp.

"Well," Hamhart said. "The hammer has fallen. Do we really need to be subtle now?"

Chapter Seventeen

DISMOUNTED

Rommond heard it with horror, and did not need to see. The carrier was overturned, and it was the generosity of fate, or its last-minute taunting, that kept it from being blown up entirely, with whomever or whatever was inside. He knew he had to change tact. There was no more room for battle. The carrier was a sitting duck, and the wolves were circling.

That was when he took the microphone for the radio and set it to a Regime frequency, even as he continued to drive, parking his landship in front of the carrier, directly in the line of fire. A few bullets knuckled the hull, but it stayed strong for now.

"Edward Rommond here," he said. "We surrender."

The shock to Regime soldiers was likely only dwarfed by the shock on the faces of Rommond's own lieutenants, most especially Myre, the gunner who sat in the landship with him, pausing between his jumping from turret seat to sponson gun. The rattle of his gunfire petered out, until all that could be heard was the general repeating those unheard-of words.

"We surrender," Rommond said.

It was a terrible gamble. The risk was very high. There was nothing more "all in" than handing over everything, yourself included. No one expected this. It was why he tried it now. It was a card he never played.

There was a moment when everything froze on the battlefield. Rommond could see his own men through the viewports, standing beside the carrier, rifles and pistols in hand, fingers stuck on the trigger. They looked around, confused. He could see the landships parked in place, or chugging to a stop. He could hear the ringing echo of the artillery, but no more exploding shells.

Then the radio crackled. It was the sound he prayed for, the only sound he wanted to hear.

"Get out of the landship," the voice said.

That was it. Not "we accept your surrender." Not "let's discuss your terms." It made him uneasy, just like his announcement made everyone else.

"You can't be serious," Lieutenant Myre said.

Rommond sighed. "Trust me."

It was funny. They would follow him into battle, without question. Yet would they lay down their guns so easily? He knew pride was a dangerous thing. Wars were lost to pride.

He pushed the hatch door open and popped his head through, well aware that at any moment a bullet could come sailing by, ending it all. This was where both sides were showing their hands.

Rommond held up his. He saw a hatch open on one of the Regime landships on the dunes, and a sniper popped out and aimed. Anyone else might have flinched or popped back inside, but the general knew that the Regime was only taking precautions. He would have done that too. He might even have fired.

Another hatch in another landship creaked open, and out popped a Regime commander, a remarkably tall and thin fellow who had no problem squeezing through the hatch, but who likely had a lot more difficult crouching down inside. He stared at Rommond through a pair of binoculars for a very long time, visibly surveying every part of him, his head bobbing up and down, stalling at the general's waist, where his pistol and revolver were sheathed.

The Regime commander took out a megaphone and shouted his orders across. "Throw your weapons out here."

So Rommond threw his weapons out, not before noting the flinching of the Regime commander as soon as he grabbed them from their holsters.

"Climb out of the landship. Slowly."

So Rommond climbed out very slowly, standing on top of the hull with his hands raised. He was an easy target now, just as much a sitting duck as the carrier was, except at least he was still standing. The Regime wanted him, without question. He just had to hope they wanted him more alive than dead. He was glad it was not the Coilhunter he was facing. He did not take prisoners.

"Jump down and walk slowly towards us."

So Rommond jumped down and made his way towards them, keeping his hands high, making sure not to make any sudden or odd-looking movements, which they might interpret as a trick or a trap. It was funny, really. He had nothing like that in mind.

He reached the foot of the box-shaped landship, where the commander kept the megaphone in front of him like a shield. It shook in his hands, and there was sweat on his brow. His shadow was stretched by the sun, making it taller and wider than him.

"Well," Rommond said. "Let's discuss our terms."

"You don't have any terms," the commander replied, lowering the megaphone.

"That's not how surrenders work."

"It is now." The commander was doing everything in his power to seem brave. His men were looking and listening. The Iron Emperor was likely looking and listening too.

As they talked, Regime soldiers rounded up the remaining Resistance fighters, forcing them out of the few landships that were still intact, before blowing them up. They did not go near the carrier yet. Rommond was glad about that.

The soldiers were ushered into a group with Rommond, surrounded by a ring of Regime men, and a ring of gun barrels pointing in at them.

"I'm not sure you fully understand," Rommond commented. "I've only given up some of my weapons. The biggest one is in that carrier over there." He nodded towards it.

"We know. It will be taken to Ironhold."

"Then go ahead," the general replied. "You'll be doing our work for us."

The commander paused. "What do you mean?"

"That carrier contains the Worldwaker."

The commander's face turned ashen. "No," he said at last.

"Fair enough. It doesn't then."

The commander took a deep breath. "You're bluffing."

"Am I?"

The commander pursed his lips. His breathing was heavier than before.

"See," Rommond said. "Would I really surrender if it wasn't to save my life? That carrier is one bullet or land mine away from blowing us all to bits. You. Me. My little sortie force and your entire army. Why, it'll take half the desert with it. We couldn't even retreat from the blast in time."

"You're lying. We know it was dismantled."

"Do you *really* know that though? See, either I'm bluffing now, or this entire surrender is a bluff. But think about it for a minute. You could have shot me by now. I took a big risk here. Would I have really done that if the risk wasn't bigger if we kept on fighting?"

The commander was sweating like a waterfall now. His collar was moist. He reached for his radio.

"They have a bomb," he spoke into it. "Is that what they were carrying?"

There was a long pause before the response came. "No. It's a missile launcher."

The commander smirked. "Good try, Rommond."

"You won't be a disbeliever for long," the general replied ominously. "We have many carriers out in the desert tonight. This is only one of them. We don't have three missile launchers. Go on, confirm that with headquarters."

The commander did, and they confirmed the details. He did not smirk then.

"So," Rommond said. "We have a few cups here. One of them has what you're looking for. But the others? What do they have? Well, I told you what this one has. It has the end of all worlds. Do you want to lift it up to look?"

"What stops us just taking you prisoner? Or taking the bomb?"

"This," Rommond said, reaching his hand into the inside pocket of his military coat. Every gun turned on him, even the turrets of the landships. He kept his hand in place, knowing he was not really holding anything at all.

"Stop what you're doing," the commander told him.

"It's too late now," Rommond replied coolly. "My finger's on the button. When I lift it off, the bomb goes off. The only person who can disarm it is safely in Blackout."

"You wouldn't—"

"You don't know what I'd do. I'm known as the Desert Hawk, but right now I'm the rat in the corner. That makes me even more dangerous than before. If I go, we all go, and the missile launcher proceeds to the Rift unhindered—if the Rift doesn't go as well."

The sun was out in force, just like the Regime, but there was not a bead of sweat on Rommond's face. It contrasted starkly with the mildew on his opponent's. He had been out of the broil of the landship's interior for long enough to cool down.

He headed back into it now, sealing the latch.

Rommond could hear a mumbled discussion inside. Though he could not make out the words, he could make out the hesitation and nervousness in every voice. Outside, the soldiers burrowed the butts of their guns into him, and he responded in kind with the barrels of his eyes.

The commander reappeared, barely giving the general a glance. "Let them go," he told his men.

They were not as incredulous at the notion as Rommond's men were when he offered his surrender. Few of them wanted to be there, cornering the rat. Everyone watched the general as if he could grow extra arms and tackle all of them at one. They watched for sudden movements, for the unearthing of a disguised dagger or hidden gun. Rommond kept perfectly still. He had already played his card.

And so the Regime forces, voluminous in number, signalled their retreat. With words alone, Rommond had turned his surrender into theirs. They left the battlefield, but even as they drove off, he could see them circling around to head towards the road that Leadman had taken. He only hoped the other general would fare better, and if he did not, that Brooklyn was not in the carrier he was unwittingly directing additional Regime platoons towards.

"Well," Lieutenant Myre said, breathing out the word with an audible sigh.

"Well indeed!"

"I didn't expect that."

Rommond worked his mouth around. "Quite frankly, neither did I."

The troops picked up their weapons and surveyed

the battlefield. They might have escaped with their lives, but that was almost everything. Their landships burned, the roofs blown open, the tracks sliced through. Some of the enemy vehicles lay in ruins too, upturned or on their side, and in the middle of it all was the carrier, still dangerously close to a mine.

"What do we do now?" one of the soldiers asked.

Rommond did not quite feel like walking. He wondered what it would take to pull the carrier back to its feet. Machinery, without doubt. If Brooklyn was there, he might be able to salvage something from the destroyed vehicles to achieve that aim. But they needed him finishing the missile launcher. They were not even certain if he was inside this carrier at all. Rommond wondered if their only real option was to check if this was the right cup. If it was, the ruse was up, and the game got harder for them. Yet it was getting harder all the same.

"I think we have an answer to that," Myre said, gesturing to the east.

Rommond did not need a spyglass for this. He could see the carriers unloading the troops by the dozen, their black silhouettes accentuated by the red sky. It was clear from their shapes that they were no normal soldiers. They wore gas masks, with tanks of oil and chemicals on their backs. These were forces ready for the fire and fumes of bombs, ones who would not so easily baulk at the general's idle threats. They jogged out into the sand, lining up in formation, guns at the ready.

The general sighed and got his ready too.

Chapter Eighteen

FLYCATCHER

Leadman's forces took the central path into Regime territory, neither the quickest nor the easiest. It kind of reminded the outcast general of the middle point of Project Trident against the Landquaker, which proved disastrous in his eyes. But this was Rommond's plan. He was the boss. For now.

The road was relatively quiet. Rommond had taken the more active route, but Leadman thought that no foray into this land could go unwatched. He hated to think that he was the distraction. After all, there was a magician on the right-hand path, and a schemer on the left.

"Well, *you* know this road," Leadman said to Commander Trokus.

"I'm a Rustport man," Trokus replied.

"Not a Mes Marana man?"

Trokus did not say anything.

"What about a loyal man?" Leadman teased.

"Loyal to who?"

Leadman smiled his crocodile smile. "That's the question, isn't it."

"I'm pledged to the Resistance now."

"Now."

"Until the end."

Leadman stared outside. "Until the end."

There was a large Regime base up ahead, dubbed Outpost Flycatcher, with huge square earthen fortifications, on which perched anti-landship guns. Thick barbed wire spread out on either side for what seemed like miles, and in front of that were the so-called "hedgehogs," metal angle beams for holding back advancing landships.

Not the hardest road, eh? Leadman mused to himself. *Just like you, Rommond, to get us to do the dirtiest work. Well, I guess it's the easy road if we surrender.*

"What do we do now?" one of Leadman's men asked.

"We have a bulldozer, don't we?" his driver, Jin, said.

"We won't need it," Trokus told them. "There's a break in the fence if we head about a mile south."

"Fine fortifications you've got here," Leadman jeered.

"It doesn't *look* like a break in the fence," Trokus replied. "The hedgehogs there are on rollers, so they can be moved easily out of the way, and then the fence disconnects if you press on it."

"Sounds a bit like Mudro's ploys. Can't say I ever had much time for them. What's the point of all this?"

"It's a route the scouts use, in case the main gate is being watched."

"Okay," Leadman said. "I want you and your men to scout that way."

"It'll be clear. Trust me."

"I don't trust you, and I won't take your word alone that it'll be clear. Prove it's clear by going through. We'll watch from a distance, and follow if everything's okay."

Trokus reluctantly agreed, and set off that way with his few troops. His loyal troops. Loyal to the Resistance. Until the end.

When they were out of view, and not even a spyglass could see them, Leadman ordered his forces to roll forward, straight up the road to the Regime outpost.

"What are we doing?" Jin asked.

"*You're* following orders," Leadman barked. "Now don't say another word."

They drove straight up to the gate of the outpost, and not a single gun fired upon them. The gate creaked open, and out strolled General Ertalak, a tall fair-haired man of around fifty. People usually did not see him, granting him the nickname of the "Stay-at-home Strategist." Yet from his normal placement in the vaults of Ironhold, he was the master planner of the Regime, leaving him with a special respect for, and a special hatred of, Edward Rommond—a loathing General Leadman shared in kind. The fact that Ertalak was out here at all would have shocked many people, but not Leadman, and not today. It was Ertalak he had discussed his appeasement with in the early part of the war.

"So," Ertalak said, "You've come home at last."

Chapter Nineteen

THE BATTLE OF FIRE AND GAS

"We have to surrender," Lieutenant Myre urge, shielding his eyes from the setting sun, which set behind the silhouettes of the approaching army. Its red glare gave a haunting aura to the troops.

"No," Rommond replied, carefully reloading his revolver. "We already used that ploy. It's not going to work again."

"I don't mean a ploy!" Myre protested. "I mean … really, we need to surrender."

Rommond's moustache twitched. The other soldiers averted their eyes.

"I'll have no more of *that* talk, Lieutenant," the general said. "Surrender to nothing. Surrender to no one. Not even Death."

"But look at what we're facing."

And he looked, as they all looked, and saw what they all saw. There must have been a hundred men out there, a hundred demons. They wore armour and masks, and beneath the masks, they wore human faces. They came in groups, some in pairs, so that they could stand back to back and spread out fire in an arc, burning all. The demons had come, and they brought Hell with them.

"Look," Rommond said. "Look, but don't baulk. Look not to shudder, but to grow more resolute. Look for weakness. Look for openings. And look to comrades, and if you do not find them, look to yourself, and to that inner wellspring of resolve that we all find in these moments."

Even as he spoke, the Regime fire-flingers advanced, and behind them came the gas-gunners, and further back the fire of the sun, and behind that the suffocating darkness of the night. Each step undid one of the general's rousing words, until he saw in their eyes their terror, and the reflection of the approaching force.

"So be it," he said. "If I am to stand and fight here alone, then I will stand and fight alone."

"Not alone," Myre replied. "I swore an oath to fight till the end."

"It's not quite the end yet," Rommond said, though he saw it fast approaching.

Myre said no more, but he stood with the general, still fearful, but resolute. Rommond saw that in him when he promoted him. He also saw the youth. He saw it more now, when he knew he was likely assigning him to his doom.

The other men took out their guns. A few mumbled half-hearted words of resolve, but their eyes betrayed them, as did the the shaking of their hands. Fear came before any advancing force, and it took out many without a single shot. If they tried to shoot back with those hands, they would likely miss.

They were eight in number, not even ten percent of the horde of leather and iron.

"We'll have to make each of us count," Rommond said. "Remember, men, we've always been outnumbered. And here we are, one way or another, ending this war."

And so the fire came.

The first jet of flame reached out over thirty metres. There was no one in its path, but it fulfilled its aim: sending fear before them even faster. The light illuminated the black armour and black masks. Even the coverings of the eyes were dark. These troops did not really need to see. They were here to burn everything.

Rommond's men split apart, spreading out as he gestured for them to take cover. They hid behind the upturned landships, but only those at the front of the battlefield. They could not retreat any further or they would leave the carrier exposed. If that was set alight, the aim of it all was lost.

Rommond used a rifle from one of his fallen comrades to make his first shot. It only had a single bullet left, with most already wasted on the mines, but it was enough. There were a lot of fallen rifles littered around the sand, and not enough hands to use them. The bullet struck one of the closest fire-flingers straight in the forehead. He halted suddenly, then toppled forward, still clutching his flamethrower. His mate instinctively unleashed a jet of flame before him, but was still out of range to hit the general.

Then the other Resistance fighters unleashed a spray of bullets into the oncoming force, killing several of them, making them look a little less daunting than they did before.

And then the gas came.

The first came in a barrel, launched from a modified artillery gun parked far back with the troop carriers, which formed a black wall across the horizon. The barrel burst open in the midst of the Resistance soldiers, swiftly unleashing a green cloud of vapour, which spread out in all directions, thick and blinding. They were now the vermin-killers, here to weed out the rats.

Rommond yanked open the escape hatch of the upturned landship he hid behind and crawled inside. On its side, it was difficult to get his bearings, but this was not the first time he was in a vehicle like this. He quickly rummaged through the debris, pushing the bodies of the driver and gunner out of the way. He was certain that there was a gas mask in there somewhere, but he could not find it. He could barely see anything. If it was not the night, which entered with him, it was the dark of the interior itself. Everything was charred from the explosion that knocked the vehicle over, even the faces of its unmoving occupants. Even the gas mask that he eventually put his fingers on. Much of it was burned clean through.

He clambered swiftly back outside, where the green cloud was expanding, and the black-masked horde was approaching. He could no longer see his companions, but he could hear periodic gunfire, along with the screams and shouts of someone, punctured by his vomiting. If he was lucky, he would vomit blood. It would be over quicker then. Yet it would never be over quick enough.

Rommond dived out into the clear air, dodging

a wall of flame that spat out from a nearby gun, and charged towards another fallen landship. That one was less damaged than the previous, but it was a lot more out in the open, in the eyeline of the fire-flingers, and not long before it was in their jet-line as well. He pulled at the escape hatch door, but it would not budge. It was buckled slightly on one side. Brute force alone would not do it, and yet he had to try. He could already feel the good air fleeing from the battlefield, not just from his frantic tussle. He could already see the sky darkening, not just from the encroaching night.

He felt a sudden heat and only narrowly missed the lashing tongue of flame that came at him. It singed the whiskers of his moustache and left little embers in the rim of his cap. As he span away, he unleashed his pistol, firing two shots. It was more than he needed, he knew, but he was caught off guard. That would get you killed. Yet, having no bullets left would do it too.

The fire-flinger crashed to the ground, almost falling into his own flame. It was then that Rommond thought to grab the gas mask from the corpse. It remained just a thought, however, because another approached behind him, and another, both alive and breathing fire.

Rommond barely had time to pull the trigger before a stream of fire whisked by him as he ran. He was forced to dive into the toxic cloud, gasping one last puff of fresh air before he disappeared inside. From there, laying with his back on the ground, he could barely make out the shapes of people and objects outside. He had to hope they were as blinded by their goggles as he was by the stinging vapour. He also had to hope they did not stray too far, because he was going on guesswork now to fire his remaining bullets.

The first clearly hit, because he heard the squelch of flesh, and the squeal of the man it entered. The second struck metal, and the third seemed to make no noise at all. Who knew what it hit further afield. The fourth—there was no fourth, he realised, as the revolver clicked idly. He was out. He knew his pistol was out too. That one he had kept track of. There were cartridges and bullet boxes in the landships. He even recalled feeling one as he searched for the gas mask, but never thought to grab it in the frenzy.

And now his breath was out too.

He gasped, feeling the first needle-points of the gas prick away at his lungs. He coughed, then tried to disguise the cough, knowing it would lead the fire-flingers to him. He covered his mouth and nose with the edge of his coat and tried not to suck in any more of the noxious fumes, but his lungs chugged along like little pumps and pistons on autopilot. If he took a breath, he would soon die. Yet if he did not breathe, he would die even swifter.

Better to burn than go like this, he thought.

So he rolled back out into the open, where he was greeted with a breath of fire.

Chapter Twenty

BLACKOUT IN BLACKOUT

The alarm did not go off in Blackout. Those who would raise the alarm were dead. Throughout the city, while the civilians dozed and dreamed, sleeper cells awoke, implementing Plan 88, silently killing off any remaining guards, taking over the guard posts and the gates, and sealing off supply routes. In a matter of hours, the city fell to the Regime, and the only people who knew about it did not know about it for long.

In the Treasury headquarters, the Baroness Ebronah was having a fitful sleep. Her four-poster bed was piled high with blankets. The cold always got to her, and it seemed to get to her more that night. She dreamed of evil things with an icy touch, and felt the frost invade.

When she awoke, something felt different. She had lived in Blackout all her life. She knew the city, and knew when it felt unwell. She had been growing more anxious as Rommond prepared to leave again. Each time he did, the city was left with a skeleton crew to defend it. The Treasury found it hard to fill the gap, no matter how much money they offered. People were motivated by the war now, by a sense of duty, and the lure of heroism and honour. You could not buy people off if they thought like that. The Resistance or the Regime got them for free.

Ebronah put on a night coat and slippers. She went out onto the balcony, hugging her arms as the icy night air embraced her. Blackout was quiet. There were times when the machinery snored through the night, but now it was silent and still. There was a sense of apprehension in the air, the kind she felt just before the Regime rolled into the streets almost a decade prior, when Rommond was forced to retreat out into the desert. She did not like feeling it now, and she wondered what might have happened to the general if this evil omen proved true.

From this vantage point, like so many other high places in the city, she could see the clock tower rising from the rooftops, its clock face stuck permanently at midnight after the building was abandoned. It was an appropriate, if unintended, symbol for the city, that twilight location that sat between both factions, and went back and forth between them. It also suggested something else to her: that the night was half over, but there was still plenty more night to come.

She saw a light on in the top window, knowing that Codex Carter and his team were working there, utilising new supplies bought with her money, preparing for Rommond's big broadcast to all Regime territory. The general had confided much in her about just how important this piece of the puzzle was. The war could not just be won with bullets. It had to be won in minds as well. The Iron Emperor could fall, but anyone could take his place, and the Iron Empire would continue. The populace needed to know that the Regime as a whole had to go.

Ebronah was lost in her thoughts when she noticed a glimmer of light in the streets below. It was faint, masked by the smog, but it worried her. The little dot of flame, maybe a torch or lantern, bobbed through the streets, winding along, growing fainter here and brighter there, as it travelled the shortest route towards the clock tower.

Fear told her that this was some attacker, but reason made her consider that it might be one of Carter's men, bringing in some extra supplies. That was not supposed to happen at this hour. She insisted that Rommond's curfew was kept, but she was not naïve enough to think that some did not break it. Yet as much as reason was reassuring, the fear did not abate.

She headed back inside, reaching under her bed to pull out a large wooden chest. She unlocked it and rooted through her belongings inside, pulling out an old spyglass, gilded along the edges. This was not a piece of military equipment, like Rommond would use, but something the Treasury had for the old safari expeditions and other luxurious pastimes that no one else could really afford.

She returned to the balcony and peered through the lens at the little bobbing oil-lit lantern, and the man holding it, and the other men nearby that the light betrayed. The magnification was weak, but it showed her enough: she could see the Regime emblem on the left shoulder of the lantern-bearer's uniform.

She rushed back inside, closing the glass-panel doors behind her and pulling the curtains shut. She clutched the spyglass tightly and breathed heavily. She did not know what to do, or who to alert.

Suddenly she heard a clamour downstairs, and she ran to her bedroom door and turned the key. She heard a thunder of footsteps up the stairs and across the landing, followed by the creaking of doors and a mix of hushed and raised voices.

She backed away, casting the key onto her bed sheets. She ran to a large oval mirror facing the bottom of her bed, catching a glimpse of her wrinkled features in the glass. She felt along the edge until she pressed down on a tiny latch, which made the mirror swing open on a hinge. She entered the dark passage it revealed, closing the false wall behind her. As it clicked, she heard the main door of her room burst open, and the bustle of boots that followed.

"Damn," a voice said. "She isn't here."

"Did she go with Rommond?"

"Of course she didn't go with him!"

"Well, where did she go then?"

Ebronah tried to calm her frantic breath, putting her hand over her mouth. She leant on the wall to her side with her other hand, and tried to step down the stairs of the dark passage. She was glad she was wearing slippers now, but still the wood creaked. She halted, and almost felt the eyes of the men in the nearby room turn towards her.

"I don't know," a voice said, "but she isn't going far. We've got the city on lockdown. No one's going anywhere."

Chapter Twenty-one

THE FOG OF WAR

Rommond gasped in shock just as much as he gasped for breath. It was not skill that saved him. It was not luck either. He heard the thunderstrike of a rifle and the whistle of a bullet as it sailed towards the fire-flinger standing dangerously close to him, so close that the assailant was in mid-spray of fire. The bullet struck him fast and hard, so hard it shoved him to the side. His grip on the flamethrower weakened mid-fall, and the darting ray of fire halted close to Rommond before being sucked back into the mottled barrel.

No, it was not skill or luck. It was Lieutenant Myre. It was having a comrade, someone to watch your back. He gave a sharp salute from across the dune. Even in his gas mask, you could tell he was really young. But with the rifle, he was as seasoned as they came.

Rommond would have breathed a sigh of relief if he had time to, or if there was air fresh enough to breathe. The green cloud was spreading. Its ghostly fingers reached out to caress him, then to choke him. He recoiled, and the gas dispersed around him, seeking out new victims to maul. In time, only he would be left, and the hands would come for his neck and lungs anew.

He scrambled across the sand, his own hands and feet periodically slipping as the grains gave way beneath him. He swiped at the face of the fire-flinger Myre killed, tearing the gas mask off. The face that greeted him was just as young as Myre's, maybe younger. If this had been the battle's aftermath and not the battle, he might have pined for him. But for now, he had to go kill more boy soldiers.

He placed the gas mask to his face for a moment to take a fuller breath. The glass in the goggles already steamed up, clouding his vision. His lungs ached and his throat was raw, as if the fire-flingers had flung fire straight into his mouth.

You're doing good if this is as bad as it gets, he thought. He could already feel his stomach start to churn. He got out of that gas just in time.

But when fighting the Regime, if you leave the cover of the gas, then the gas-gunners come for you. Rommond had barely managed to fill his lungs when he caught a moving shape from the corner of his eye. He had to pull the mask away to see more clearly, and he saw the gas-gunner with his mutant-shaped mask and bloated backpack, striped across the top with a horrid bisque-coloured paint.

The gunner fired, and Rommond barely got the mask back to his face in time as a yellow chemical sprayed from the gun. The eyelets clogged up with it, and Rommond felt a terrible blistering sensation on the hand that held the mask. He was blind and he was burning, and all he had now were his fists to fight with.

So he fought.

He simultaneously pulled the mask away to see, while his right fist swung in an arc to meet the cheekbone of the gas-gunner. He heard and felt the crunch, but the pain in his left hand helped distract from the right. He threw himself at the man to prevent him firing the acid again, knocking them both to the ground, where the sand leapt away in little yellow clouds of its own. The general bashed at the face of his attacker. It helped that he wore that ugly crow-shaped mask, because it made him look like a monster. He certainly spat venom like one. Rommond made sure he spit blood too.

By the end of it, the gas-gunner put up no fight at all. Rommond's fists were bloodied from the bashing as well as the corrosive spray. He pulled the gloves off the dead soldier's hands and put them on, gritting his teeth as the leather rubbed across the frayed and blistered skin. He glanced around to see if there was another attacker, but all he saw was the growing cloud of gas. He swapped his acid-laced mask for the crow-shaped one. It extended over his entire head, so he had to get rid of his cap as well. He immediately noticed a huge improvement to his sight and breathing. This had been purposefully designed for close-quarters immersion in this chemical spray. He noted that the man's coat was made of a similar material, so abandoned his own for that as well. It felt odd to be wearing Regime attire, especially something as ill-fitting and uncomfortable as this, but it was not the first time he had done it. He hoped it would be the last.

The final piece of the puzzle was the backpack and the attached gun. He heard the liquid slosh around inside as he hauled it into place. He did not have a mirror, but he was sure he looked the part. Any discrepancies would be covered by the green fog.

He stalked through the sand and the smoke, hearing far-off gunfire, and wondering just how far he had strayed from the main fight. He still saw the husks of landships, and here and there a body, and every so often a gun. He took up any pistol he could find, checking it for ammo. Many were out. That's why the people who held them died. A few had a single bullet left. He had no time to take out the bullets and put them all into a single gun. He hoarded all of them in the pockets of his new black leather coat, hearing them clink off one another as the leather squeaked.

Suddenly a group of five gas-gunners marched through the gas ahead of him. Instinct almost made him fire, but he stopped in time. The acid from his gun would do little against these fiends, and there were too many of them for his bullets, and not enough strength left in him to take them on with his hands alone.

He gestured to them, pointing further into the masking vapour, as if he had spotted someone inside. He tried the right measure of confidence and fear for someone who was on the trail of General Rommond, as if they almost had a shot, but were afraid he almost had one too. They must have bought it, because they spread out around the location he pointed to, and three of them went cautiously inside. The other two waited outside with Rommond, all three of them with a slight shudder in their guns, but only one of them was faking it.

With one hand still holding the gas gun, he reached with the other into his pocket, pulling out a pistol. With the speed of a hawk darting towards its prey, he unloaded the bullet into the head of the man to his left, while spraying acid at the man to the right. He knew the latter would not kill him, but it blurred his vision a little and distracted him for just long enough for Rommond to take out a second gun.

Yet before he could fire, he heard another gunshot, and soon after felt the stabbing pain in his leg. His leg buckled, and as he fell to his knee he glanced around to see Lieutenant Myre's head bobbing down behind one the landships.

Damn it, Myre! he thought. *Look before you shoot.* He was only glad that his aim was off this time. What cold irony it would be to have been saved by Myre, only to be killed by him moments later.

It should not have been a surprise, but the Regime soldier Rommond had just sprayed ran to him to help him up. As he did, the general realised that he must have thought the spray was an accident from all the gunfire, and that the bullet that struck their other companion also came from Myre's gun. The disguise was working—perhaps too well. It seemed he was now inadvertently fighting on the wrong side.

He and his new comrade trotted off into the safety of the green cloud, keeping close together, side by side, watching each other's backs. On many occasions, Rommond considered taking out another pistol, but then his knee would cave, and the Regime soldier would help him up again. The soldier was short, probably more of a kid than all the others, and his hands shook a lot more noticeably too.

God, the general thought. *How did you get caught up in this?*

For a moment, he wondered if he was asking it of himself.

They continued through the gas, hearing more gunfire in short rattles, and more roaring flame in long gushes. All the sounds set the other soldier's hands shaking even more, until Rommond was forced to pat him on the back for reassurance.

It'll be all right, he thought. *You'll be dead soon.*

Chapter Twenty-two

BENEATH

Whistler felt the first glimmers of consciousness, accompanied by the first prickles of pain. His head throbbed. His muscles ached. His ears rang out fiercely. The screeching noise was constant for what seemed like forever, then slowly started to fade. As it did, his vision returned, though it returned blurred.

Am I dead? he thought to himself, wondering if the dead could think. The second thought he buried: it was about his mother, and it was more painful than the physical sensations running through his body.

He realised he was staring up at a stone plinth overhead, far up, so high up that he thought it had to be more than six feet. He thought maybe it was the crust of the earth, and he was in the centre. His mind raced with the ideas, dragging the next one over the last, like a burial tomb, until it seemed they tripped over one another, and his mind was a jumble, foggy and distant.

For a moment he lay there, until he realised he could feel some of the stone beneath him too, a little cold in places, and quite hot in others, where the spears of the sun poked through to sear the surface. Yet he also felt something different beneath his head, like a pillow, and something a little coarser in his hand. He turned his head very slightly and looked down at his hand, only to realise that he was still clutching Jacob's, or rather that Jacob was still holding onto him.

Then the fog cleared a little, and he remembered the rolling column, and the horrible fall that followed. He felt it again in the pit of his stomach, as if his organs were plummeting. He felt the wind catch his breath, stealing and silencing his cry. He saw the rush of colour, the tumble of ground and sky, the blurring of all things, and Jacob's body dropping like an anchor with him.

He recalled hitting something, and feeling a stab of pain in his left ankle, before it seemed that he was sliding again, and Jacob was sliding faster. He thought they both reached out with their other hand for something to grip, and both looked up as the column came down upon the new, smaller slope, still intent on crushing them.

Then they fell again. What little breath he had sucked in was torn once again from his lungs, and the sight became even blurrier, and the sounds became even harder to distinguish from the taunting whistlers of the wind. It seemed like a longer fall now, and he felt and heard the thump of the impact for barely a second before a rush of tingles leapt up through his body, as if to counterbalance the fall. Once it struck his head, the tingles became sparkles in his eyes, little growing stars upon a black field. And then nothing.

He felt a different kind of tingle now in his feet, and he found he could wiggle his toes. There was a sudden sense of immense relief in that little movement that somewhat frightened him. He did not like the idea that he had even considered that he might have broken them beyond repair. As he glanced down towards his feet, he saw the shattered column that had plunged after them. It had not fared so well.

He found it difficult to concentrate, and had to bring his attention back to his feet, and then to his hand, and then to the hand he held, before he could focus once again on the smuggler. *Jacob!* his mind erupted, and the lava of his thoughts caused his headache to worsen.

It was a struggle to move, to shift in the gravel, feeling every little grain burrow into him, punching and prodding at the bruises, the sand stinging like salt at all the little cuts and grazes. He could feel the tears in his clothes, and the blood, some still wet, some already clotting. He could even see one of his shirt buttons dead in the sand a little to his right, its gossamer entrails all hanging out.

Again he found his mind distracted, and it was as much of a struggle to refocus as it was to move. He rolled around, still feeling Jacob's coarse fingers in his, still feeling the pillow of the smuggler's torso beneath his head, and still feeling the probing gravel. But the rolling made him think of the column tumbling after them, and he felt once again the churning of his innards, the stealing of his breath, and the blurring of his eyes.

It was the sudden sharp pain in his left ankle that tore him back to the present. Then it all settled, and he was on his belly, his head and shoulders resting on Jacob's chest. He ushered himself up, still clutching

Jacob's hand, as if suddenly he might feel that fall again.

Then his grip weakened as he saw Jacob's body, still and silent, bruised and bloodied. There was a large gash across his forehead, oozing blood. It ran like a waterfall down the side of his face, gathering in a pool on the ground below.

He could not see Jacob's chest rising and falling, and he felt a sudden intense guilt that he had been lounging on the smuggler's chest, possibly preventing him from taking a life-saving breath. He realised that Jacob had, for the most part, broken his fall. He could barely contend with the thoughts of what Jacob had broken.

"Jacob," he whispered. It was an urgent whisper, and maybe he meant it as a cry. The gravel was in his throat as well, punching and prodding there too.

There was no response, not even the slightest of twitches. The only thing that moved was the blood, still trickling away.

Then the urgency of the situation kicked in, and Whistler realised he needed to act fast. He wished he had paid more attention to what Lorelai showed him in the infirmary, or what Mudro had showed him years before.

He let go of Jacob's hand, which fell back down into the sand with a crack. It was a horrible sound. Whistler tried to tear off some of the straggles of his torn shirt, but was not strong enough to rip them through. He dangled them over the wound on Jacob's forehead, then pressed them down, sapping up the blood, pressing as hard as he could to staunch the blood flow.

He wondered what Rommond might do in this situation. He remembered his words in the clouds when they chased the Worldwaker. *Keep to the mission.* He wondered what that meant for them now. Keep to it how? He even questioned for a moment if the general would have left Jacob behind.

But he would not.

He tried with all his meagre strength to haul Jacob up, only to collapse down with him with a thud, his ankle stinging and swelling. He panted from the effort, well aware that if the roles had been reversed, the smuggler would have whisked him up with ease. He cursed his boyish arms, with no bumps on his biceps, and wished he could have grown up faster and been of more use.

In that moment of resignation, when he thought it all was futile, he thought again of Rommond's words, and realised there was still a way to keep them. *Keep to the mission*, the general had told them. But the mission had changed. Now, for Whistler, the mission was getting Jacob out of that ravine alive.

So he stuck to the mission, clambering up again, and crashing down again, and trying it all over, ignoring his own pain, until he found that he was making tiny advancements up the slope, more from the collapsing than the carrying or hauling. It was exhausting work, and he was glad that for now he was in the safety of the shade.

He only hoped that by the end of it all, if perseverance paid off, he would not find that he had just dragged a body from its grave.

Chapter Twenty-three

THE CLEANSING

R ommond continued his careful prowling through the lime-coloured vapour, sometimes wafting it away with his hand as it grew thick around him. His Regime companion still strolled with him, and his hands still shook violently, especially when there was a sudden sound of gunfire nearby.

The general could still feel the pain of the bullet in his thigh, just above the knee. He limped, and hated that he limped, not just because it was painful and embarrassing, but because it would make him stand out to anyone watching—or anyone shooting.

Then they bumped into two fire-flingers, who were making a circle around the battlefield, burning almost anything that moved. The oil tanks on their backs released a foul smell, which mingled with the even fouler odour of the gas and acid, and seemed to seep even through the leather of Rommond's mask. God only knew what it was like for those without one. Yet men knew too. Rommond stepped over one of them, one of his own, with the vomit still wet upon his face, the blood still rolling down from his crazed and widened eyes.

He let the fire-flingers pass, as they were heading

away from where the battle still raged, if the gunfire could be trusted. Rommond had a saying for that: *You can trust gunfire to give you away*. Right now it gave away the position of one of the remaining Resistance fighters.

He hurried over to the location, followed swiftly, and a little too closely, by the youthful Regime soldier. It was one thing to know someone who had your back; it was quite another to have someone cling to it.

He saw one of Myre's cadets peeking out from one of the viewports of an upright, but disabled, landship about a hundred yards ahead. He could not remember the cadet's name, and probably never learned it in the first place. He memorised the names of people who survived long enough to be promoted. Too often he had to forget them again soon after.

The cadet was careful with his shots, which suggested he was low on ammo, or had heard the general's saying before. Hiding inside the landship seemed like a good idea, as he was walled off from the world, well shielded, but clearly the young soldier had not heard another of Rommond's aphorisms: *In a battle of fire and gas, make sure you're in the open.*

Rommond saw another two fire-flingers approaching from the side, outside the vision of the viewport, drawn by the rattle of bullets. He charged forward, gritting his teeth through the pain, and his Regime companion galloped after him. The fire-flingers only had to walk, only had to stick the nose of their flamethrowers through another viewport of the landship, only had to pull the trigger.

The landship's interior lit up like a furnace. The

cadet's scream was blood-curdling. It almost drowned out the sounds of his fists bashing against the metal, of his desperate attempt to get outside.

Rommond slowed to a stop and tried hard not to shake his head. He watched as the fire-flingers passed him by, almost seeing the smile in their eyes through their fogged-up goggles. It took a special kind of person to join the Burning Unit, the kind that not only wanted to watch the world burn, but hear people scream. From the growing trembles of the youth beside him, he clearly was not one of them. His knees knocked together as if he had been shot worse than Rommond.

There was gunfire far to the right, so Rommond raced towards it once again, but the sounds died off before he even made it close. He had to clamber up the side of a dune, with his fellow gas-gunner supporting him, to find the dead Resistance soldier on the other side.

It was Lieutenant Myre. He was burned to a crisp. The only identifying mark was the golden coin hanging from his coat pocket. It was lucky all right, because it had survived the fire. But not its owner.

Damn it, Rommond thought, but no one could damn it any more. This was the bottom of the barrel, as far down as he could go. This was Hell. This was war.

Well, if this is Hell, then let everybody burn!

He took up Myre's fallen rifle and checked how many bullets were left. A glint caught his eye, and he saw half a dozen bullets half-buried in the sand near the lieutenant's blackened hand. He never got to load them in time.

Rommond perched himself on the top of the dune, like a hawk upon an eyrie. The other soldier knelt down with him, laying his gun on the sand. No doubt he was the type who never wanted to hold it in the first place. There was not the hint of residue on the barrel.

From this vantage point, Rommond could see much of the battlefield, and the toxic cloud that hung over it. His eagle eyes caught the movement of figures in the haze, and his talon fingers caught the trigger of his rifle.

This time he did not go for the head. The two fire-flingers who had burned the cadet were passing around again, and they turned their backs to Rommond, revealing the oil tanks. He fired just one bullet, which burst through one of the tanks and lit him and his companion ablaze. It took a special kind of person to join the Burning Unit, but they burned and screamed the same.

Another bullet took out a second patrolling duo, and it seemed that the gas itself caught alight, spreading like wildfire. The whole place lit up, highlighting other patrolling figures inside. There were a lot of them there, and not enough bullets for them all, so Rommond made his careful calculations and fired a ricochet shot off one of the landships, which took out half a dozen.

The Regime soldier to his right shifted in place, surprised. He picked up his gun and backed away, but he never fired it. If he had been any other soldier, he would have fought Rommond. If he had been any other soldier, he would be dead.

Rommond continued his lightning-fast blasting of the enemy, until all his bullets were spent, and no one moved in the haze below. He knew his own companions were already dead. He had counted them as he stepped over their bodies. He did not count the enemy. He had killed too many.

With the battlefield cleansed, all that remained was the general and the new recruit.

Rommond stood up and pulled off his mask, and the Regime soldier panicked. He seemed unsure if he should fire or run, or soil his pants. If he stood there during an earthquake, he would not have shook as much.

"Put the gun down," Rommond told him.

Still the soldier did not know what to do.

"Put it down, boy."

The soldier complied, as if Rommond was his superior. In war, he was.

"Take off the mask."

The soldier pulled off his mask, revealing a teenager's face beneath, maybe fifteen or sixteen, his messy hair pasted to his blemished face with sweat, his eyes wide with terror, his lip trembling with it too.

Rommond shook his head and sighed. "I'm supposed to kill you, you know."

That did not help the soldier's trembles.

"That's what war is, boy. You've seen it up close. Did you volunteer? Were you conscripted? I noticed you never fired your weapon. This isn't for you, is it? Well, boy, it's not for anyone. It'll ruin you. So, go. Get away from here. Get away from this."

"Y-y-you're letting me g-go?" the teenager asked.

"Yes, boy. Call it one good deed for a hundred bad ones."

"And y-you're not gonna shoot me in the head when I t-t-turn around?"

Rommond humphed. "I've done that before, but no, not this time."

The soldier was incredulous. "So you're not the monster they said you were."

"Oh, I am," the general replied. "It takes two devils to make a war."

The teenager had no words to reply to this, and barely had the wits to turn and run away. He clearly did not know where he was, because he was running west, into Resistance territory, where he would be imprisoned. Yet, it was probably wiser than running back to Regime land, where he would be shot for desertion.

Rommond sat back down on the dune for a moment to rest his limbs. He tore off the Regime coat and rolled up his sleeves. He bit into the wooden casing of the rifle, then dug his fingers into the wound on his leg, until he pulled the bullet out. He took his canister of water from his belt and cleaned the wound. He took the other canister of whiskey and cleaned his soul. He used what remained on his leg as well, before wrapping it tight with a torn strip of his trouser leg. He was not entirely sure if his unkempt uniform bothered him more than the gunshot wound.

When he had rested for long enough, which was not long at all, he hauled himself up and looked back down to the battlefield, where the gas was clearing.

The numerous bodies could be seen a lot clearer now. Sometimes it was easier to fight in the battle than witness the aftermath.

Then his eyes turned to the carrier, what this fighting was all about. It sat on its side for the entire battle, largely outside the arena, a spectator to it all. He was only glad the fire-flingers had orders not to fling their fire inside that too.

He hobbled down to the carrier, careful to watch for nearby mines. He spotted the one dangerously close to the hull, now partially covered by sand again. That was dangerous. Sometimes a single grain could set them off.

He looked at the huge hatch door on the back of the vehicle, and knew he had no other choice. It was time to see what was under the cup. With the carrier on its side, it took a huge amount of force to open it, the kind of force Rommond did not feel he had. Yet, with the thought of Brooklyn trapped inside, he found new strength buried behind his heart.

The hatch opened suddenly and Rommond fell backwards into the sand. From there he could see inside the carrier, filled only with the battered remnants of one of Brooklyn's earlier prototypes. It might as well have been empty.

He had little time for despondency, however, as he heard the now-familiar thrumming of engines and saw the always-familiar cloud of unsettled dust coming from the north. It seemed the battle was never over. There were just small interludes.

Chapter Twenty-four

A GIFT

At Outpost Flycatcher, General Ertalak rapped a knuckle off the carrier. "You've brought us a gift."

Leadman smiled. "Consider it a … friendly gesture."

"It'd want to be, what with your constant flip-flopping."

"I go where the tide goes."

"Well, it's good you think the tide goes this way." He paused. "Do you know what's in it?"

"One of Rommond's prized weapons, of course."

"Not a bomb?"

Leadman furrowed his brow. "No."

"Rommond's carrier had a bomb, last we heard. Quite a big bomb, actually."

"That wasn't the weapon I heard about."

"Seems you might be out of the loop."

"One more reason not to fight for Rommond, huh?"

"Certainly."

"So then, I expect you'll keep your end of the bargain."

"You can have Blackout for all we care. The real

bastions are in the east, and those will stay in maran hands."

"That's fine with me."

"Probably more than you'd get with Rommond."

"Yes. That's why I'm here."

"So, shall we open it up?" Ertalak asked.

"Sure."

"Why don't you do the honours?"

"Why me?"

"Well, let's just say we've had enough booby-trapped carriers pass into our hands over the years. The so-called Order used to leave them lying around and issue fake reports of amulet finds."

"Well, the Scorpion won't sting any more," Leadman said with glee.

"Maybe not," Ertalak said, "but the venom stays for quite a while."

Leadman forced open the large back door of the carrier, and the panel fell down with a clang. They peered into the dark inside, illuminated only by a faint oil lamp. They saw a huge vehicle on gigantic landship treads, with several crystal missiles on its hull, and several more piled on the floor nearby. Half-buried in the cockpit hatch was Brooklyn, pausing mid turn of a bolt with spanner in hand.

Ertalak could not contain his laugh. "Oh, Leadman," he said. "You can have every city in the west for this. You said one of Rommond's weapons. You didn't say the maker of them."

Chapter Twenty-five

CONVERGENCE

Whistler collapsed into the sand with a sigh. He could drag Jacob no more. The smuggler's arm fell limp when he let it go. It was a horrible struggle, but at least Jacob's body stayed in place, unlike the last few attempts, when it slid back down a metre or two, adding more work to the next terrible haul.

Whistler sat up, resting his arms on his knees, and his chin on his arms. He felt the scorching sun on his back, burrowing through the fibres of his already ragged shirt. The setting rays fell also on Jacob's face. At first, Whistler moved until his shadow gave the smuggler some shade, but then he thought maybe the sunlight would wake him up. It always did for him, when they were not fighting this ugly, evil war.

"I'm not strong enough," he said aloud, glancing at the paltry muscles on his arms. He had tried copying the military exercises Rommond ordered for his troops in the morning, but he could never keep up. He barely managed a few hours before giving up from exhaustion, and he had to rest for a week to recover from it all. He berated himself now for not keeping it up, for giving up so easily, for not better preparing for something like this, for a time when he would be tested.

He gave a tiny shrug. "I guess I failed," he told himself. "No wonder they never wanted me to come on missions." His memory was barbed, and one of the thorns was a word his mother had used for him: *liability*.

Yet, as he sat there staring at Jacob, his memory returned something a lot less stinging: some of Jacob's words, those comforting, encouraging words that lifted him up when he felt he was falling down. It made him think again about what Jacob would do. He would not give up.

"I have to get stronger," he said, standing up, grimacing from the pain in his ankle.

He grabbed Jacob by the wrist and dug his heels back into the sand, then leant back with his entire body weight until he could pull the smuggler up the dune just a little. It was agonising work. He had heard people say they would "feel it in the morning," but he could feel it now. He did not want to think of what it would be like tomorrow. He was not so sure the two of them would survive the night.

It was another hour of this, with barely much progress, before Whistler noticed a figure approaching. He knew it was not Mudro or Nox. He had already hobbled up the dune and around to the top of the bridge to look for them, screaming for the doctor to help. They had already left long ago. This other figure was different. In Regime territory, that could not be good.

In any other circumstances, it would have been Jacob who took the lead, ushering Whistler behind some cover, preparing to fight and win. Now it was just him, alone and defenceless. The panic of it all almost overcame him. He scampered back and forth a bit, unsure what to do, before spotting the pistol strapped to Jacob's belt. He grabbed it and hid behind an outcropping, crouching down, holding the pistol with both hands, thinking it felt rather heavy, thinking it looked huge and clumsy, thinking maybe he was not strong enough to shoot. He closed his eyes and tried to calm himself. He let the metal on the top tip his forehead and recoiled from the blistering heat of it.

The figure approached, spotting Jacob in the sand. When he reached the smuggler, Whistler could better make him out. His head and face were covered in some kind of tan-coloured head scarf, which extended down to cover his shoulders and upper arms as well. He carried an overflowing backpack, and he leant on a walking stick. Whistler did not know what to make of him, but he was prodding Jacob with the stick, and that was enough for him to act.

He leapt out, waving the gun before him. "Get back!" he cried, his voice breaking mid-shriek. He felt he could barely hold the gun. He could barely hold himself up either.

The man backed away, holding up his hands. "W-w-woah now!" he said.

"I mean it," Whistler said, but he did not really. "I'll shoot."

"N-n-now, boy, d-d-don't be a—" The man cut himself off mid-sentence. "Brogan? Is that you?"

Whistler's mouth dropped. It was about as much

as he could manage for a response.

The man unwrapped his head scarf, revealing a familiar face: that friendly, wizened, harmless face of Uncle Alex Cotten, with his unkempt brownish-blonde hair and round, brass spectacles.

"Uncle Alex?" Whistler asked, even though he knew the answer.

"Brogan!" Alex cried. "What in the D-d-devil's name are you doing out here?"

Whistler looked down at Jacob. "Trying to save him."

"Well now," Alex said. "We can d-do something about that, can't w-w-we?"

Whistler nodded.

"M-m-maybe put down the gun?" Alex suggested.

Whistler had half-forgotten he was still holding it. He was just glad his finger was far from the trigger. He let it droop in his hands and tried to hand it to Alex, but his uncle backed away, holding his hands out in protest.

"N-n-no, not me!" he said. "I can't t-touch one of those. I'm a p-p-pacifist through and through."

Whistler knew that already, and had asked him about it before on one of their few archaeological digs together so many years ago, before Alex went off into the east to make greater discoveries in Regime land, and was presumed dead by the Resistance. He remembered the arguments Taberah and Alex had, and how they did not get along because of how staunchly they disagreed about the war. He even remembered helping his uncle fake a doctor's report to avoid conscription, and he certainly remembered the anxious dreams he had for months after that of the Resistance taking him away in the middle of the night to punish him for his heinous forgery.

"Oh," was about as good as Whistler could manage now, before putting the gun down on the sand beside Jacob. "Can you help him?"

"I can t-t-try," Alex said, unloading his backpack. He pulled a water canister out and dribbled some over Jacob's face, before taking a swig and offering it to Whistler. The boy gulped it down and poured some over his hair, letting it drip refreshingly down his face. He suddenly felt the sun more now, as if it had been hiding in his skin. The light was fading, but the air was till hot and humid.

"You should p-probably wear this," Alex said, handing him a straw hat that was strapped to his backpack. Whistler put it on, feeling a sudden immense relief in the shade it offered. He knelt beside Jacob's head, letting the hat shield his face too.

Alex took out a variety of things, including an aloe vera ointment, which he rubbed gingerly on the cut across Jacob's forehead, and a flask of smelling salts, which he waved frantically before Jacob's nose. The smuggler did not stir.

"That usually does it," Alex said, scratching his head.

"Can you not do more?" Whistler pleaded.

Alex bit his lip. "I'm not a d-d-doctor."

"We have to do—" But Whistler froze. He saw several half-tread trucks speeding through the desert straight towards them.

Alex heard the thrum of the engines. "Oh God."

"We have to hide him," Whistler said.

"Where?" Alex cried. "He needs m-medical attention!"

It was then, just as Whistler grabbed the gun again, that the boy noticed the white flags billowing from the roofs of the trucks, and the white crosses emblazoned on their hulls. He saw the sun setting behind them, and realised they must be coming from the west, from Resistance lands. At least, he hoped they were.

"I think they're ours," he said.

"Ours?" Alex asked. As far as he was concerned, his side only had one person on it.

The trucks pulled up close, halting nearby. They could see several nurses inside. Two of them leapt out with their medical supplies as soon as they saw Jacob on the ground. One of them, to Whistler's surprise, was Lorelai.

"What happened?" she asked, rubbing her hand across his face quickly before she tended to Jacob.

"We fell."

"We need to get him out of this heat."

She inspected his head and neck for any signs of serious injury before they hauled him into the nearest truck. The nurses crowded around him, stripping his shirt off.

Alex tutted at Whistler. "Women."

They bathed the smuggler down, cleaned out his wounds, braced his broken arm, and applied much stronger smelling salts than the ones Alex had. The archaeologist leant cross-armed against the truck with the air of "I could have done that."

When Jacob eventually stirred, he was in a daze for quite a while. They gave him water, and eventually he was able to speak.

"What's your name?" Lorelai asked him.

"I don't remember."

"Who is the head of the Resistance?"

"I don't know. You?"

Lorelai shook her head. "What day is it?"

"Hell," Jacob said. "I don't think I ever know what day it is."

"Do you remember anything?" she asked him.

He grinned. "Everything. But it was fun to play."

She rolled her eyes. "This is serious, you know. You could have died or had a brain injury."

"Just an average day then."

She rolled her eyes and hopped outside, where she found Alex and Whistler chatting. Alex hushed himself when she approached.

"It's okay," Whistler said. "She's one of us. You can trust her."

She eyed the explorer up and down. "You don't look like the fighting type."

"Oh G-g-god no!" Alex cried.

"So why are you out here?"

"Well, I'm usually looking for my next dig site," the archaeologist said, "but this time I did a little surveillance work for Rommond, as a kind of way to … umm, p-p-pay my respects." He avoided looking at Whistler, and avoided mentioning Taberah by name.

"Surveillance?" Lorelai inquired. "Surveillance of what?"

"That Rift the demons use. Sure, I know its

patterns of movement like I know the Great Caverns of Talgyroni. Rommond wanted me to help g-g-guide Brooklyn when he got out here in his new … vehicle. I thought these fellows m-might've been him, actually."

"So you're still on your mission," Lorelai said.

It was then, and only then, that Whistler noticed the gun strapped to the nurse's belt. He had not seen her with a weapon before, but then he thought maybe he was not looking. Something about it struck him as odd, but he dismissed it.

"Yes," Alex said. "The Rift has settled for now. I'll need to find Brooklyn quick if I'm to show him the way."

"Maybe we can join you," Lorelai suggested. "The more, the merrier, right?"

Chapter Twenty-six

BEHEMOTHS AND BASTIONS

On the southernmost path, Mudro continued on, weary. The Coilhunter looked like he was born weary, so it made little difference to him. They drove slowly, carrier and monowheel side by side, wondering how they would ever fight with such diminished forces.

"This must be some weapon," Nox said, glancing up at Mudro from beneath the rim of his hat. "It's killing us off good."

Mudro sat on the roof of the carrier, cross-legged, feeling the old injury that made him limp acting up again. He said nothing. There was little to say. He had seen Whistler grow up. He never thought he would see him die as well.

They crawled along, careful and watchful, far slower than they needed to be. Mudro did not want to admit it aloud, but that was because he was waiting for backup. It seemed that some of the landship platoons that went out into the desert never arrived. He wondered if they met a worse fate than his group.

Dawn was breaking once again. Mudro had gotten very little sleep, waking regularly to find they had barely made much progress, or that he had dozed for only minutes at a time. When he glanced at the Coilhunter, the weathered bounty hunter seemed wide awake, still puffing smoke through his mask, like Mudro wanted desperately to puff the mind-relaxing leaf. It did not seem like the Coilhunter ever slept at all.

The emerging sun revealed the path ahead: the Dune Burrows, those gargantuan mountains of sand, etched and carved by the fingers of man, the muscle of maran, and the ethereal touch of the weather. Giant slabs of limestone stood like the dragon's teeth the Regime built around Ironhold to ward off an advancing army of landships. Yet these must have been from a bigger dragon for a bigger army, for they towered over even the huge carrier Mudro perched upon.

"Nature," the doctor mused aloud.

"It'll kill ya," Nox replied. He never said it, but when so close to the Coilhunter, there was always the implication of: *If I don't kill you first.*

"Not an outdoors sort?" Mudro asked him.

Nox was silent.

"Well," the doctor said. "It'll be some trek up there." He pointed to a colossal set of granite steps far in the distance, which must have been even more colossal up close.

"Why not go around?

"Because of that," Mudro said, pointing to the top of the stairs, where a swirling lightning cloud formed.

"More nature," Nox grumbled.

"No," Mudro said. "That's the Rift. That's the doorway into the demon world."

"Let's get knockin' then."

They continued across the dappled landscape, chasing away the shadows as the sun rose slowly, but as they neared some of the gigantic dunes, falling under their own enormous shadows, they started to see what the night had been concealing: a series of hastily-made fortifications dotting the dunes, and the hulls of Regime machinery jutting out from behind pillars and blocks.

Mudro signalled a halt, and both the carrier and monowheel stopped fast in the open. From there they could more clearly see the Rift, growing and shrinking, spinning and casting out scorching blades of lightning. They were so close, but there were a lot of obstacles in the way.

"If we turn, they'll know we've seen then," Mudro whispered. He was not entirely sure why he whispered. They were far from earshot, and far enough, he hoped, from gunshot too.

"Oh, they know," Nox said. He did not whisper. The grit was still in his throat, as if a desert existed there too.

"I don't have magic for this."

"We've got metal," Nox said, pulling his rifle from his back.

"They've got metal too," Mudro said.

He did not need to point. No one could miss what they had missed at first. The ground shuddered, and one of the immense dunes to their right seemed to crumble apart. As the sand and rock gave way, the iron beneath awoke. Dust was replaced with the smoke of many furnaces, and the gentle sound of the breeze was replaced by the clang and clash of metal. It was a Behemoth, a towering rectangular-shaped monstrosity of industry, supported on huge metal tracks and iron columns, which tore apart the land like it was an enemy.

"You don't have magic for that, do you?" Nox asked.

"We're going to have to run."

Nox looked back at the huge distance they had come, and the lack of cover anywhere. All the cover was ahead, with the enemy. There were two-legged Moving Castles there too, hiding behind that cover, and those could move faster than any landship could. If it was just the monowheel, they would be fine. The carrier made everything difficult. It made everything deadly.

"We're not gonna get far," the Coilhunter said.

The sandy cliff to the left shuddered, and they knew there was a Behemoth beneath it too.

Mudro sighed. "We're not going to get far with fighting either."

Then something else caught their eyes to the north, emerging over one of the smaller surrounding dunes. For a moment it seemed like a wall of black, until Mudro strained his sight through a spyglass to see the details. On the left were dozens of diesel-powered bikes, upon which sat the remaining members of the Oxen clan and the Copper Vixens, led by their new Copper Matron, a purple-haired woman with more tattoos than clothes, but less muscle and mass than their previous leader. On the right were dozens of tribesmen on horseback, the Dust Riders, some just now emerging from a dying dust devil that gave this fast-moving force some cover. It was only then, as the sand began to settle, that Mudro saw another welcome sight: General Rommond in the centre, wearing a borrowed cap and coat, and standing half-submerged from the hatch of a Mark III landship. Behind him, and behind them all, were dozens more vehicles of all shapes and sizes, one of the largest reserve forces sent out into the desert, now reunited for a final fight.

"I'm hopin' that's backup," Nox said.

"It is," Mudro said, amazed. "Some luck at last."

Nox grumbled noisily. "Don't trust in fate or hope yet," he said, pointing his rifle south, where there was another black wall forming. "Those your boys too?"

Mudro turned his eyeglass in that direction, but it was clear in an instant that they were not another Resistance platoon coming to join the battle. There, lined up as neatly as Rommond would have had his finest soldiers, were at least a hundred members of the Iron Guard, half-man, half-machine, and altogether deadly. It was backup all right, but backup for the Regime.

And in the middle of these three huge armies sat Mudro and Nox, spotlighted by the sun, and the valuable carrier they were trying to defend, parked on the doorstep of victory, but not yet close enough.

Chapter Twenty-seven

GOLD AND GLAMOUR

In Blackout, many were scared to look outside. A curious few felt the same fear, but looked out anyway.

Porridge opened the door of his room in the Olive Inn and peeked through the gap.

"Hello?"

There was no response.

He crept downstairs, hearing the sound of his heels striking the wood like a gavel, so he scampered down the last few steps in a hurry, as if doing it faster would somehow mask the ruckus.

He saw a shadow in the main room moving back and forth, so he grabbed the nearby potted plant and waited by the door to strike. The shadow approached, and its owner came through.

"Crikey!" Gus called out when he saw him, shotgun in hand.

Porridge's shriek almost broke the glass.

"What're you doing down here?" the landlord inquired. "And what're you doing with me plant?"

Porridge placed it back on the table delicately. "Just making sure it's watered."

"Fine time for gardening," Gus said. "There's a

war out there."

"Oh, I know!" Porridge said. "Isn't it dreadful?"

"I mean here, in the city."

Porridge grabbed the wall for support. "Tell me you're not serious, silly."

"Wish I weren't," Gus said, cocking the shotgun. "Them demons've gone and taken over."

"Does this mean Rommond failed?"

"Doubt it. More likely they're taking advantage of him not being here."

"Well, what do we do?" Porridge asked, biting his index finger.

"We bloody well fight is what we do," the landlord said. He started off again, but Porridge grabbed his shoulder.

"Wait!" the trader cried. "These shoes aren't designed for battle." He raced upstairs in his six-inch heels with a clamour of gods fighting, then returned with a slightly diminished discord in three-inch boots, and, of course, a matching scarf.

"Now I know why women don't go to war," Gus said.

Porridge raised an eyebrow. "Whatever do you mean?"

Gus handed Porridge a second shotgun. Then they headed out the back, and as they did they heard the radio come on. Gus turned and fired, blasting a hole in the wall. Out rolled the clockwork construct Bitnickle, with her constantly-switching radio frequencies for a voice.

"Don't ... shoot," she said, the first word from a broadcast on what Regime citizens were obligated not to do, and the second from supposedly live coverage of the slaughter of Resistance forces at the hands of the valiant Regime superiors.

"Come along, Bitnickle!" Porridge said.

Gus grumbled at the wasted bullet. "You should've made her with a gun."

The Baroness continued her scurry through the tunnels, careful and quiet, but as fast as she could possibly go on her aching limbs. She feared it was only a matter of time before the Regime forces discovered the secret passages, and any hope of overcoming them would be lost.

She took up an oil lantern as she passed, chasing away the shadows as she went, until finally she arrived at a locked cellar with a golden keyhole. She produced the matching key from her bosom, and the ancient door creaked open far louder than she liked.

She entered.

The room was dank and musty, and her high-worn grey-white hair caught in the cobwebs. This was an old room for old things. She could not help but think: *and for old people*. It was where some of the vestiges of the bygone royalty were kept, the relics of rulership. They were now mostly symbolic, but they were kept out of sight from the monarchy's successor, the Treasury, because there was nothing more symbolic than money.

She held the lantern up, until its faint light bounced off the many golden items within. It was a huge cellar, with Regime-outlawed paintings on the walls, and dusty books, and many ornate chests and tables, and display cabinets full of precious things.

On the wall facing the door, up a series of steps like those of a throne, was a large wooden plaque. Displayed upon it was a golden musket, which was to the Baroness the most precious thing of all. It was the only thing in the room that was not dusty, the only thing she came down to this room of memories to clean. It belonged to her husband.

She placed the lamp on a nearby table and took the gun down slowly. It was heavy, thanks to its gold plating. It was not really designed to be used, but it worked all the same—not that it had been tested since her husband's death. He had been a gentle soul, who saw Blackout through many troubles, caring for its people as if they were kin. It was fitting, she thought, that he would play some part in the defence of the city.

She took down the other items hooked to the plaque: a gold bayonet attachment and a box of paper cartridges, with pre-measured amounts of gunpowder, and, of course, a golden ball as a bullet. In this war, so many people had died from iron. She would use gold instead.

Chapter Twenty-eight

CANYON CHASE

At Outpost Flycatcher, Brooklyn barely had time to duck back inside the missile launcher's cockpit before the bullets came. He heard people clambering on the bonnet, and just managed to shut the hatch door before they reached inside. More bullets came, but this vehicle was meant for them. It was just a shame he had left so many of his own crystal ones behind.

Brooklyn fired up the engine and hammered his foot on the accelerator until it hurt. The Hometaker bolted out of the carrier and rammed through the two landships ahead. He could barely see through the viewport, letting the shutter close periodically as the bullets pelted his way. Then he cleared the Regime base, blasting through a wooden palisade and flattening a wall of wire with barely a scratch upon the giant tracks.

He used every trick and technique Rommond had taught him, and every whispered word from the machine spirits, to give the missile launcher as much speed as he could muster. The sand erupted in his wake, barely settling before it was thrown sky high again when the Regime vessels came in pursuit.

No matter what he tried, they gained on him. They were smaller and lighter vehicles, and they did not have to support giant Glass missiles on their hull. He needed more speed, but no amount of shovelling coal would give it to him. He had already overfed it. The vessel belched black smoke.

The landships behind began to fire. He heard and felt the patter of gunfire on the hull, and the sharp clang as a bullet caught between the tracks and was crushed between them. He tried swerving left and right, but the bullets followed, and then the landships split into a line of three, dividing their fire to cover his constant movement.

He turned sharply to the left when he saw a dip into a canyon below, letting the steep slope hasten his flight. This crevice was only wide enough for one landship, so it forced the enemy to go single file again. As he glanced in the mirror, he could have sworn he saw the bulldozer landship of General Leadman leaving the convoy and heading out into the open desert.

The bullets came anew, but now he had the natural twists and turns of the canyon to aid him. He followed the winding path, barely slowing for a turn, letting the vehicle crash through overhanging rocks and scrape off jutting formations. The bullets still struck the hull now and then, but many more were wasted on the stone walls.

Then he heard a sharp whistle and saw the larger shells of turret fire in the one side mirror that was not already shattered with gunfire. One of the shells hurtled past, striking the rock face ahead, sending the splintered stones down on top of the missile launcher and into its path. With his vision blurred by the debris, Brooklyn had to rely on instinct, and with his advancement blocked by that same debris, he had to rely on brute force. He had already been giving it his all, so he had little left to give. The vehicle crunched and crushed the smaller rocks, knocking aside the larger, and all of this slowed it down considerably.

And then more shells came, and these struck one of the Glass missiles, shattering it into a thousand tiny shards, which rained down on the vehicle and the ground around it. Brooklyn continued on, aware that he had only four missiles left. If he had not been forced to flee so soon, he might have had more.

There was some brief reprise, however, when the Glass shards caught in the tracks of the landships and wheels of the trucks pursuing him, slowing them down as well. Even destroyed, the missiles were a weapon to be reckoned with.

The snaking path continued, but it grew slimmer and tighter the further they delved into the canyon. Brooklyn glanced out of the viewports on either side, looking for a break in the cliff walls, but there was nothing to be seen. Then suddenly he thought he saw a turn, but he drove so fast that he missed it. The next one he saw was but a mere crack in the surface of the wall.

So he continued on, but the crevice became even smaller than before, until he could hear and feel the vehicle bashing off one wall and then the other, and only hoped those few millimetres of space would remain or he would scrape off both.

He spent so much time looking for an escape on either side that he barely noticed the sudden squeezing of the cliff walls ahead, which tapered off into a point. There was no way the missile launcher would fit through. Even a person would have found it tough. It was only the blinding sunlight outside that showed there was even a break in the walls at all.

Brooklyn knew what Rommond would do, and spared no time in doing it. He fired one of the Glass missiles straight ahead, which exploded through the rock, raining grains of sand and particles of dust. The hole it formed was big enough for him to get through, but it was also big enough for his pursuers, who came hot on his tail, tracks still spinning, guns still blazing.

The Hometaker leapt back out into the open, where the sun came suddenly through the viewports like a flood. Brooklyn grabbed his goggles, but even as he did, he caught the sight of something approaching from the right. By the time he saw that it was Leadman's bulldozer landship, it already struck. The force of it sent him flying, and sent the missile launcher rolling onto its side, then its roof, where another missile shattered, onto its other side, and then back onto its heavy tracks again, where it rocked for a moment as the dust settled.

Brooklyn lay on the floor of the vehicle, battered and bruised, giving out a faint moan for the not so faint pain throughout his body. He was dazed, his vision blurred, his head spinning, his stomach churning. It took a moment for it all to settle, and even in this confused state, he knew he did not have a moment to spare.

He heard the revving of an engine, which made him more aware of the smell of coal and oil of his own vessel, and of the burning embers of the fuel that had spilt out from the furnace in the tumble. Then he heard the increasing chugging of turning tracks, and knew that Leadman's bulldozer was making another charge.

He tried to clamber up and brace himself, catching sight through one of the viewports of the approaching bulldozer blade, only to see another landship—driven by Commander Trokus—crash straight into the side of it as if it was a bulldozer as well. Leadman's vehicle was caught suddenly and sent skidding off to the side, and Brooklyn's second tumble was averted.

As he heard the engines kicking off again outside, and what sounded like muffled shouts and spot gunfire, Brooklyn tried to focus on what he needed to get his own vehicle moving again. He found the shovel under his seat and lobbed a pile of coal from the floor into the furnace, where the flames were quickly waning. He turned the engine on, hearing it cough sickly in response.

"If ever I needed machine to work, it is now!" he said aloud in frustration. He did not have the time or patience, or the right frame of mind, to commune with the machine spirits, and hoped his little verbal plea was enough—and hoped it would not offend them either.

He pressed buttons, pulled levers, spun cogs, and tried everything he could to get the missile launcher moving, increasingly aware of the growing battle outside, and his own place in the middle of it all. The bullets did not seem to be aimed at him yet, but some of them still belted off the surface in the crossfire.

Then suddenly the Hometaker jolted forward and the engine kicked into action. He stomped on the accelerator and the tracks span anew. The vessel sped off into the rising and falling dunes, leaving behind many of the landships, though some of them started the pursuit again. He was not entirely sure where he was going, and looked to the sinking sun for guidance. He only knew he was leaving the battle, and hoped he was not heading into a new one.

Chapter Twenty-nine

THE BATTLE OF IRON AND OIL

The Regime made the first move. From behind every pillar and wall came a Moving Castle, and from over the highest dunes emerged a fleet of landships. They stepped forth and rolled forward, engines purring, steam spewing, guns blazing.

Rommond's army swept in next. The bikers revved and the horsemen charged, working up the sand into a cyclone. The Oxen clan and the Copper Vixens zoomed down into the plain of battle, and the landships followed, with the general still visible from the hatch, issuing hand signals amidst periodic glances through his spyglass.

The Iron Guard came last, springing down the dunes on their machine legs, with their machine balance keeping them upright. Each of them was modified in a different way, some with metal limbs, others with eye implants, and others still were almost the complete iron package, with just a few human or maran organs left inside their metal shell. Their ligaments were pistons, powering the rapid movement of their legs, and their veins were wires, powering not only the circuitry that tied them together, but the variety of weapons that protruded from their arms and shoulders, or replaced them entirely.

Amidst all of this, these three tidal waves of iron and oil, Mudro and Nox sat in the middle, bracing themselves. There was no more time for flight, and plenty of bullets in their guns.

"Now I know why I stay outta this," the Coilhunter said. "I ain't no warrior."

"Well, you better become one," Mudro said. "This is war."

Nox attached the rifle from his back to the side of his monowheel, before reaching into the supply box of the vehicle to pull out three more. He attached these in a similar manner, until he was left with two rifles stuck to either side, all locked and loaded, and all within reach when he climbed onto the seat and revved the engine.

"See ya out there," he said, before flicking the black portion of his sheriff's badge. "There's a bounty on these demons tonight, and I feel like cashin' in."

He sped off, straight towards the advancing Regime force, the monowheel gaining speed, cutting a path through the sand, and swerving and tilting as the bullets came flying his way. He leant down low, both to duck the barrage and help him accelerate even more. Before anyone knew it, he shot between two oncoming landships, evading their turret fire, and they barely had time to halt and turn before he was gone again, and before Rommond's force came in from the side.

The turrets boomed, and between their thunderous percussion was the faster rhythm of machine gun fire, and the patter and pelting of metal, and the rending and puncturing of steel. Some landships exploded on the spot, and others kept rolling as the fires blazed within them. Tracks were unthreaded, hulls were unhinged, and rivets fell to join the bullets and spent cases in the sand.

To Nox's great surprise, the Iron Guard did not attack him, and did not attack his comrades either. They went straight for the Regime vehicles, climbing them, sawing holes in them, blasting through them. He had heard rumours of Brooklyn's experiences in the east, but he never quite believed them. He did now.

The Coilhunter continued his passage through the mayhem, taking pot shots at opportune targets, drawing fire away from Mudro's rolling fortress in the middle, distracting the enemy from Rommond's approach on their flank. He zoomed through, finding now that the bikers and Copper Vixens were doing the same, engines barking, exhausts fuming, and gun barrels bellowing. So too came the Dust Riders, galloping fast and working up a blinding wall of sand, making it difficult for the Regime snipers to find their targets. Some fell, horses tumbling beneath bikes, and bikes rolling through the sand as their drivers were knocked off dead. For every one that zoomed through unscathed, another was caught in the maelstrom.

Nox pushed on, for as the battle burst to life in the plains below, the first Behemoth continued to burst through the rock and sand that buried it, taking its first fateful steps towards the fray. It could crush all, friend and foe, and keep on crushing. To Nox, this was at the top of his *Wanted* list.

* * *

Mudro dived and rose from the hatch on the top of the carrier's cockpit, lobbing grenades out into the fracas, while the driver below piled up some more and pulled the pins on them one by one. His throw was good, and the explosions ripped the legs off Moving Castles, sending their crew plummeting, or tore holes in the sides of landships, or blew their turrets off completely.

"We're running out," the driver called from inside.

Mudro lobbed the last few, then ducked inside again, closing the hatch behind him just as a riderless horse tried to leap over it to escape the fray. It was dark inside, almost pitch. They had closed the viewports and sealed every door. It made Mudro wonder just how dark it was for Brooklyn in the back—if he was even there. Now it almost did not matter that they were defending the Hometaker, or keeping up the ruse; it mattered that they kept the carrier intact for their own survival.

"Is there anything else we can use?" the doctor asked.

"Not really," the driver replied. "I think we should save the bullets from our pistols. They're not going to do much against landships."

A sudden explosion shook the carrier.

"I think we should get this moving again," Mudro suggested.

"It'll mean opening some viewports."

The bullets pinged off the surface, even the hatches of the viewports, as if to remind them that the metal desperately wanted to get inside.

"No," Mudro said, holding up his right index finger. "I think I can drive this blind."

They swapped seats, and Mudro turned on the engine. Then he set the gear to reverse, and backed up, and kept backing. They bumped off something, then heard the crashing of a Walking Castle, with the distinctive droning of its iron limbs. They struck the edge of something else, larger, like a landship, which might have been one of their own. Then they felt the crunch of debris beneath the carrier, and then the smoothness of the open sand again. He kept on backing up, relying on Rommond's eagle eyes to spot them, and do everything possible to wall off the enemy from coming after them.

General Leadman let his fury guide him. He heard the Regime reports of the battle waging at the Dune Burrows, and so he turned his forces in that direction. General Ertalak's platoon went with him, and from the back of Ertalak's landship hung the battered body of Commander Trokus, his legs dragging across the ground. He would never see his family again, and they would not want to see him—not like this.

"A bit grim, don't you think?" Leadman had asked Ertalak.

"He's a traitor."

Some might say I am too, Leadman thought. He did not like that it bothered him. He was in too deep now. He had to go all the way.

They had long lost track of Brooklyn and the Hometaker, thanks to Trokus' intervention, but as they approached the battle at the Dune Burrows, they spotted something fast approaching: another giant Resistance carrier, backing its way swiftly through the desert.

"Another one?" Ertalak asked through the radio.

"Three of them set out," Leadman explained.

"Does *this* one have a bomb?"

"I doubt it."

"Then why are they driving away? I thought they had a weapon?"

"You *saw* the weapon they have. It's a missile launcher."

"Then this one must be more valuable. They're trying to escape."

"Not this time."

Leadman drove straight towards it, and the carrier continued its backwards flight, until they met with a clash, and the bulldozer blade scooped up the carrier and pushed it back, until it toppled over completely onto its roof.

The landships circled around it, even as some of Rommond's forces broke off from the main battle further ahead and made for their location.

Leadman and Ertalak got out.

"Open it up," Ertalak ordered.

Several soldiers set dynamite around the huge hatch door at the back, which blew it open with a boom and clang. When the dust fell, all they saw inside was just another prototype, a mere shell of a vehicle. Anything that could be salvaged from it had already gone into the construction of the Hometaker.

Ertalak was furious. "What sort of game are they

playing?"

They blasted open one of the cockpit doors, dragging Mudro and the driver outside, kneeling them down in the circle of vehicles, like a sacrificial pit. Rommond's forces still advanced towards them, but there was still a great distance between them.

"What's the meaning of all this?" Ertalak asked, gesturing to the empty carrier.

"I'm as surprised as you," Mudro said.

"I doubt it," the Regime general commented. "You're the magician, aren't you?"

"That's right," Leadman confirmed.

"This another of your tricks?"

"We call it Thimblerig," Mudro said with a smile. "You picked the wrong cup."

"No," Ertalak replied. "*You* were in the wrong one."

He fired his pistol, and Mudro collapsed, leaving a growing pool of blood around his head. There were no magic shields for bullets. The lead disappeared into his skull.

"Run," Ertalak told the driver.

So the driver ran, and the general shot him in the back.

"Now," he said, pulling a comb out of his coat pocket to tidy up his hair. "If we're going to play games, I see that Rommond is approaching. Let's have a Game of Generals then."

Chapter Thirty

HUNTING PORTALS

"**M**ind taking it easy?" Jacob begged, as the medical truck leapt down deep descents and shot up steep hills, rocking and shaking the entire way. He held his hand to his aching head and tried to ignore his motion sickness.

"Maybe we should slow down," Whistler suggested, biting his lip and surveying the smuggler with worried eyes.

"Keep this speed," Lorelai ordered. "We need to … rescue Brooklyn." It was odd to hear her barking orders in this context. She usually only gave them in an infirmary. Jacob thought that the Regime's strictness must have rubbed off on her.

"We've got a navigator to the the Rift," Jacob said, "but we could do with one to Brooklyn. Do we even know where he's supposed to be? Or where he was last seen?"

"I know," Lorelai said, stretching over him to turn on the radio. She kept turning the dial until she rested on a strange Regime channel, which sounded like a very boring broadcast on Regime dress code.

"Maybe something Rommond would enjoy," Jacob quipped.

She shushed him and listened closely.

"I know where he is," she said at last. "He's coming south along the Canyon Coast."

"How do you know that?"

"It's a codemasters channel. Everything they say is in code."

"And you know that, how?"

"It's standard Regime training."

Jacob glanced around for someone else to confirm, but they all shrugged.

"Fair enough. So, where's this Canyon Coast?"

"Here," she said. "Let me drive."

She took the driver seat and turned them around, heading north-east, while the rest of the medical convoy continued on their designated route. They continued on for several miles, until they finally caught sight of a vehicle speeding through the desert.

"That's it! That's him!" Jacob cried. He recognised the design from Brooklyn's schematic. He was just glad he had been trusted with seeing it, or they might not have known at all.

Initially, Brooklyn steered away. He must have thought it was another Regime vehicle chasing him. Then Jacob and Whistler hung out of the windows, waving frantically, and he eventually rolled to a stop.

The truck pulled up beside it and everyone bar the other nurses got out. Lorelai told them to go ahead, that the dying needed them, so they bundled up their belongings and headed off again, seeking out war's leftovers.

The door of the Hometaker creaked open.

"Finally," Jacob said, running his hand across the

buckled hull. "What took you so long?"

"Hurry! Get inside!" Brooklyn replied. He reached out and grabbed Whistler's arm, pulling him into the cockpit. Jacob, Lorelai and Alex squeezed in after. It was a tight fit. Most of the vehicle was made up of the firing mechanism.

"Cosy," Jacob said as he rubbed shoulders with Lorelai. He felt someone rubbing off the other shoulder and turned to see Alex there, beaming.

"Quite!" the archaeologist said. "Reminds me of the t-t-tombs of the Treasury ancestors. You'd find maybe five bodies like this, crammed into the same g-g-grave. Marvellous stuff, really."

Jacob raised an eyebrow. "Yeah. Marvellous."

"Now then," Alex said, unfolding a gigantic map, and banging off Jacob several times in the process. He extended it out, blocking much of their view. "We should be … hmm."

"Hmm? That doesn't sound good."

"Ah, there we go," Alex replied, unfolding the map even further. He pointed to a series of markings in a straight line across the desert in the east, culminating in the Dune Burrows. "This is where the Rift, for want of a better word, *travels*."

"Pity it wouldn't come to us," Jacob remarked.

"And here," Alex continued, gesturing to a large empty space on the map, "is where we are … more or less."

"More or less?"

"M-m-maybe more or maybe less. It's not an exact science."

"Doesn't sound like a science at all."

"Well, we're roughly here, give or take a f-f-few miles, and the Rift is currently here at the Dune Burrows. We've got a couple of hours left, I'd wager, before it starts to move again."

"Dune Burrows," Brooklyn mused aloud. "I know there."

Alex smiled broadly. "Yes, by chance. What luck!"

"Not chance. Not luck, no."

"Maybe it's fate," Lorelai said. There was something about her that was a little odd. She seemed more steely than before, more like a soldier on a mission. Jacob supposed that saving people's lives was a mission of its own, and she was clearly dedicated to it. He never thought to take notice of the lack of medical supplies she brought with her.

The Hometaker travelled along the quickest route to the Dune Burrows, forgoing the dusty concrete roads and dustier dirt tracks for the empty expanse of the desert, where the miles could not be counted by anyone who still had their sanity.

"I see it," Brooklyn said. "I see Rift in sky above."

Jacob peered out, glancing left and right until he caught sight of the swirling mass of cloud and colour, of flashes of light and sudden outpourings of dust. It hung above the gigantic dunes with their immense constructions, and even from this vantage point it looked like it was too far up in the sky to pass through.

"Let's hope these missiles work then," Jacob said.

"Yes," Brooklyn replied. "Let us hope."

Jacob scrunched up his mouth. "I was kind of hoping you'd be a bit more certain than that."

"There is nothing certain now," the tribesman

said. "Except maybe death. Yes, big battle ahead. Death is certain."

Chapter Thirty-one

PRISON BREAK

"What can you see?" Gregan asked.

Tardo strained on the tips of his toes, but still could not quite reach the small barred window in his cell.

"You're taller than me," he replied.

"Yeah, but I'm not the one with the window view." Gregan rapped his knuckles off the wall.

Tardo had to resort to jumping, and even then his eyes barely reached above the sill.

"There's some kind of … commotion."

"We know *that*," Gregan complained. "We can bloody hear the commotion!"

"Something to do with the clock tower."

"Must be Rommond's doing. I heard some of the guards talking about odd supplies going back and forth there."

"They don't look like Rommond's people."

"What *do* they look like?"

"Well … one of them is wearing an Iron Empire—uh, I mean *Regime*—uniform."

"Your pals, eh?"

"No, definitely not. I'd be shot if I ever went back."

"Maybe you should go back then."

Tardo rolled his eyes. He sat down, cross-legged, and sighed. "Guess there's nothing we can do. The city's being overrun, and we're stuck in here."

"Well," Gregan said, drawing out the word, and seeming like he was on two minds whether he should say anything else.

"Well what?"

"There might be a way out."

"There might be a way out?"

"Yeah. But if I tell you this, you need to come back here and free me."

"Eh, okay."

"Dig around there in the corner."

"In the corner?"

"Of your cell."

"There's nothing there."

"Trust me. Dig around a bit."

Tardo complied, feeling around the floor. "There's nothing—oh. Oh, wait." He felt the edge of something. At any other time he would have thought it an uneven tile on the floor, but if he dug his nails in he could feel it move. With some careful pushing and pressing, he managed to lift the edge of the secret hatch door.

"Wow," he said. Then he paused and looked at Gregan. "You knew this was here the whole time?"

"Yeah."

"And you didn't tell me?"

"I don't exactly like you, Tar."

"*Tardo*."

"Yeah, I just dug you a tunnel out of here. I'll call you what I want."

"Fair enough. Do you know where it leads?"

"No," Gregan said, "but the boy came through it, so presumably somewhere safe."

"Taberah's boy?"

"The half-breed one."

"That's the one. Well, I mean—"

"Are you going to stay here yammering or are you going to escape?"

"Oh, yes."

"Well, go then. And remember, you promised to come back for me."

"I will."

"You better."

"*I will.*"

And then he disappeared into the tunnel, racing about in the dark frantically, feeling the walls as he went, and eventually ending up in the old butcher's shop. As he pushed open the hatch door, he heard voices in the other room.

"I'll only be a minute," one of them said. It sounded like Royce, the butcher.

There was a muffled response which Tardo could not make out, but it was clear they were annoyed.

"Go on without me, you maggot, and I'll follow you down!" Royce barked back.

Tardo clambered through the hatch as quickly and quietly as he could, only to find Royce wandering into the room.

"Now where did I—" He halted, blinked at Tardo, then reached for a cleaver on the wall.

Tardo glanced around, pulling the lid off a crate just in time to use it as a shield when Royce charged forward and sliced down at him with a shout. The cleaver embedded in the wood, and cut through just enough for Tardo to see the sharpened blade on the other side and shriek in response.

"I've seen great big rats crawl out of there before," Royce roared as he tried to pull the cleaver out, "and you're the biggest of them all!"

He slammed his other hand on the back of the cleaver, as he often did for particularly tough cuts of meat, and the wood snapped in two. Tardo cast the parts away and reached out for anything and everything, firing old bottles, rags, and even scraps of meat at the butcher as Royce swung and swiped like crazy.

"I, uh, I ..." was all Tardo could manage to utter as he pushed a crate out in front of him and danced around it with his cleaver-swinging partner.

"I know who *you* are, Tardo," Royce replied, "you traitorous little rat. There's posters of you. Wanted to start your own little resistance, eh? Wanted to be taken under the Hawk's wing?"

Tardo made a dash for the door into the main room, and Royce hobbled after him. Tardo reached the front entrance and pulled at the knob, and twisted it, and pushed, and fiddled, but it was jammed.

"It's locked, you idiot."

Royce's cleaver came down hard on the door, and Tardo dodged it just in time, but lost his footing in the process, landing on his back. He scurried away backwards, banging his head off the counter. He looked around, but saw nothing he could use as a weapon or a shield.

Royce reefed his cleaver free of the door, pulling a large splinter of wood with it.

"You know there's a shortage," he said with a hint of glee. "Not many farms left in this world. The pigs and cattle are hard to come by." He yanked the wood from his cleaver. "Sometimes I've got to use the rats."

Tardo closed his eyes and held his arms up above his face, bracing for the end.

Then he heard a loud blast, Royce's winded grunt, the thud of the butcher's body off the floor, and the clatter of the cleaver that followed. Tardo sat up and prepared for his turn next. Then a head popped through the large hole left in the door, and it was Porridge with his golden curls and outrageous multi-coloured bonnet.

"I got him!" Porridge cried ecstatically. "Oh, my word!"

His head popped back out, and then the door burst open, and in strolled Gus, shotgun in hand. He stood over Royce's body. "Never did like the chap," he said. "Used to overcharge me, he did."

He helped Tardo up. "Glad to find you here. We need the reinforcements."

"There's one more," Tardo said, "back at the prison."

"We'll be passing that way."

"On our way to where?"

"Where the action is!" Porridge exclaimed, waving his own shotgun around. "I'm locked and loaded, and up for anything! Oh!"

"And you?" Gus asked. "This is a do or die moment, this."

"I'm ready to do," Tardo replied, "and ready to die."

Chapter Thirty-two

THRESHOLD

The Hometaker drove along the cliff road at the top of the Dune Burrows, making straight for the Rift, while the battle continued to rage in the plains down below.

They came within firing distance, and Brooklyn parked the vehicle. Far ahead, near the Rift itself, they could see the open-topped warwagon of the Iron Emperor, and the man himself was there, radiating his presence, gazing on all with his transfixing eyes.

"It is time," Brooklyn said. His finger hovered over the button.

The anticipation was great, and Jacob wondered what would happen when the missile launched. If the door opened, who would walk through? What would they find there? What dark secrets did the Iron Emperor want to keep locked away? A part of Jacob, and a part of them all, did not want to know.

Suddenly Lorelai struck the tribesman on the back of the neck with the butt of her gun, knocking him out. He slumped down and fell from his seat, his iron hand clanging off the floor.

"What are you doing?" Jacob cried.

"Back away!" she responded, aiming the gun at

him. "All of you, out!"

Alex needed no encouragement. He leapt outside, pulling Whistler out with him. Jacob stayed behind.

"I don't understand," he said.

"This plan is a mistake," she replied. "If you topple him, who will help us find the cure?"

"*We* can help you."

She shook her head. "I wish it was that easy, but he's our only chance."

"So, what, you're just going to let this war keep on going?"

She bit her lip. Her eyes watered. "You don't know what it's like, that *disease*."

"Then tell me."

"I can't. I can't begin to describe what it's like, to see someone you love fall apart, until there's nothing left of them. To have to lie to them to tell them they'll be okay, that they'll get better, that the pain will go away. He promised us a cure, Jacob, and when we ran out of iron in Mes Marana, and there was not enough Hope left to treat my son, I promised *him* I would find a cure. I didn't find it in time for him, but I still have to look. It's why I came here as a Pilgrim, and why I have to see this through."

"And what if it doesn't end like you thought it would?"

"Well," she said with a sigh, "it'll end, at least."

"I thought you were supposed to save people, not hurt them."

"I'm trying, Jacob."

"And what if *he's* not? I said it before back in Blackout. What if he's not looking for a cure? What if that's just to string you all along, keep you placated while he takes over another world?"

"But what if he *is* looking," she replied. "I can't take that risk. He's far from perfect, but he's the best chance we've got. If anyone can find this cure, it's him. I know he's looking. He has to be."

"Why?"

"Because he's got it too."

"He looks fine to me."

"Many of us look fine, but we're dying all the same."

"You know I have to stop you," Jacob said.

"I was hoping you wouldn't say that. I don't want to hurt you, Jacob."

"Well, too late for that. You know I kind of trusted you."

"I'm sorry, Jacob, but you've got to put yourself in my shoes. This wasn't an easy decision to make. Now, go. Get out."

He would not budge. It was no longer just his usual defiance. He felt he had to do something for the greater good now. He could almost hear Taberah's encouragement in his ear.

"Please, Jacob," Lorelai pleaded. She sounded as earnest as ever, and yet Jacob was not sure if that too was a ruse. "I *will* shoot you. I don't want to, but I will. I've been *trained* to do it. It's in my blood."

"Come on, Jacob!" Whistler called from outside. Jacob did not doubt the boy's earnestness. The worry was clear in his eyes. Yet, again, Jacob felt he could not simply let the Regime win. He had to do something, or die trying. The latter option seemed increasingly likely.

"Don't be a hero," Alex added, keeping out of line of sight.

A year prior, Jacob was anything but a hero. Now, he felt like he did not have a choice.

He reached for the firing button and slammed it down, only to grimace as she fired a bullet at his hand. The missile launched, zooming across the sky, while Jacob pulled his bloodied hand back, stifling a scream. The look of horror on her face surpassed his own, and he thought that she would unload every bullet into him, and search for more, search for ammunition with as much determination as her search for the cure. She kicked him in the chest, knocking him out of the vehicle, just as the missile struck the Rift and exploded, starting a chain reaction that began to widen the portal.

"You fool!" she roared, and he prepared for another bullet, and for the end, but she did not fire. Maybe it was shock that stopped her, or maybe she had not always been feigning compassion. She looked more confused than ever, more conflicted.

The doorway to the other world continued to open, until finally it was big and close enough to step through from the highest pinnacle of the Dune Burrows, that same plateau where the Iron Emperor sat in his open-top warwagon, watching the battle unfold. His attention was now seized by the Hometaker and the Rift. He quickly issued orders to his commanders, and they got inside the warwagon and drove through the portal with a demonic haste.

"Haven't you wondered what you'll find?" Jacob

shouted up at Lorelai. Still she kept the gun pointed at him. Still she kept her finger on the trigger. "Haven't you wondered at all?"

She looked at him and then at the Rift, and set the vehicle in motion. Jacob clambered up and grabbed a hold of the side of it, but with one broken arm and one punctured hand, he fell off a few feet further up as she gained speed. Regime soldiers fired upon the missile launcher, but she broke through all the barriers, until she passed through the final one and entered her home world for the first time in fifteen years. What she would do there, and what she would find, was anyone's guess. Jacob thought it would not be good.

Chapter Thirty-three

A GAME OF GENERALS

Rommond's landship platoon continued its advance, with the general's own vehicle in the lead.

"It looks like they have the carrier," the gunner said.

"That doesn't matter now," Rommond replied. "Brooklyn's not in that one." He had seen the missile launcher racing across the highest cliff of the Dune Burrows to the dwindling doorway to the maran realm. "We need to keep this army here, away from the Rift."

"What about the others?"

"They'll have manage without us."

Rommond picked up the radio microphone. They were built into all the landships, but seldom used, thanks to the Regime's constant listening. Radio was one of the Regime's great successes, helping them organise, aiding their surveillance and propaganda. He hoped, in time, it would be their downfall.

"Desert Hawk here," he spoke into the microphone. "Formation Arrowpoint."

Outside, the platoon shifted until they formed an arrow, with Rommond being the stabbing top. It was a classic formation, tried and tested, a kind of fallback in uncertain times. It would strike hard in the centre, pushing straight through, diving the enemy in two. It had the power to break morale, to route armies, to force surrender, but only if the enemy was not prepared for it.

The combined forces of Ertalak and Leadman were initially assembled in a long strip, but on hearing Rommond's voice over the radio, they knew exactly how the Resistance leader would deploy, giving them time to react in kind. Even before they saw the finished product of Rommond's formation, Ertalak issued his counter with Formation Arrowshield, a rectangular block in the centre, designed to take the brunt of the central push—to, as it were, blunt the tip of the arrow. They would advance as well, shield pushing out to meet arrow, to blunt it all the quicker.

Ertalak laughed. "You do know we're listening, right?" he called into the radio, picking the frequency the Regime spies knew the Resistance used.

There was no reply for a moment, and Ertalak imagined that Rommond was panicking. He hoped to hear his voice, to hear that waver, that hint of doubt. When the enemy general eventually answered, just as the arrow point was coming close enough to strike, there was none.

"I'm counting on it," Rommond replied, as assured as ever.

Ertalak then felt a moment of doubt of his own, the kind other generals had told him about when they faced the Desert Hawk on the battlefield, and a feeling he was glad he had never felt before, thanks to his role as the "Stay-at-home Strategist." Now it was his turn, and he only hoped that Rommond's apparent confidence was just a bluff. You could never tell with Rommond. He never seemed to do what you expected.

Then, as the turrets readied for their first tremendous volley, Rommond's platoon suddenly split apart. The arrow vanished into the haft, and the haft itself divided in two, spreading out wide enough for the opposing force to drive straight through. All of Ertalak's first turret shots missed, hitting the empty air between, and the force of their acceleration kept them moving through, even as Rommond's forces halted and turned on the spot, with Brooklyn's enhancements making them turn much more quickly than their Regime equivalents.

The end result, which Ertalak could barely comprehend, for he was in the thick of it, was two strips of landships on either side, pointing in, and Ertalak and Leadman's forces driving straight down the middle of it. Every single one of them showed their vulnerable sides, and not a single one of their turrets pointed at an enemy vessel. They could not even stop or turn, for the only unblocked path was the route ahead, that tunnel of death they had driven straight into.

Then Rommond's platoons fired. Shells tore through the Regime landships, incapacitating them, starting fires and boring holes. The path ahead became even more deadly, for landships in the middle now crashed into the stalled vessels of their comrades, and then those behind them, until there was a pileup of vehicles, and others swerving and dodging, their frantic gunners falling around inside. A few of them managed to turn their turrets to make a paltry answering shot, but few of Rommond's landships fell, and when they did, there was another behind it, and it drove forward, pushing the ruined hull into the already narrowing path of the Regime forces, before sending yet another round of turret fire into the fray.

Ertalak was caught amongst it all. He barked to his lieutenants, screamed into the radio, and pleaded to whatever god he prayed to. No amount of shifting gears or firing of sponson guns would help. He too went up in the blaze that consumed his vehicle.

The few landships at the rear of the shield formation who had not yet advanced into the tunnel turned in place and tried to flee. One of these was Leadman, in his distinctive bulldozer landship. It was then that Rommond broke off from his group with a handful of others and began their chase. They followed them out into the desert, and around high stone formations in this obstacle-ridden part of the world.

At one point it seemed they lost them, for they turned sharply around the edge of a plateau. When Rommond pursued, he was caught off guard, for Leadman had stopped fleeing and was parked there, ready to face him. He advanced, crashing into the side of Rommond's landship, knocking it over. The other Resistance landships fired on it, while the remaining Regime vehicles continued their flight from battle. Though punctured by gunfire, Leadman backed up and charged again, turning Rommond's landship onto its roof. He was about to come in again when a final shell from a turret tore the tracks off one side and set the bulldozer landship alight.

As Rommond broke free through the escape hatch of his vehicle, Leadman leapt out of his own and made a dash into the desert.

"Really?" Rommond called after him, before lining up a shot. He could have went for the head or the heart, but he chose the leg. Leadman slumped into the sand with a cry.

Rommond strolled out after him, finding the other general attempting to crawl through the desert, like a crocodile desperate to find a lake.

"It's a long way back to Copperfort," Rommond said.

Leadman halted and rolled onto his back. "Damn you, Rommond."

"Damn me? You're the one who sold your soul to the Devil."

"You were never going to honour our agreement."

"Honour?" Rommond asked. "You shouldn't use words you don't understand."

"You could have won this war with my help."

Rommond scoffed. "You could have been a decent person, but this is how the dice fall. You can't keep re-rolling if you don't like the result."

"My choice kept the citizens of Copperfort safe for *years*."

"And my choice," Rommond said, as he pointed his gun, "will keep them safe for many years to come."

Chapter Thirty-four

GO BIG ...

The battle continued in the Dune Burrows, and the Behemoths finally joined the fray. Their great limbs stomped on landships, and their great tracks flattened others like a steamroller. Inside their angular hull, machine gunners prepped their weapons, and then unleashed the sputtering gunfire through small hatches dotted along the surface. The chassis of many Resistance landships were buckled and then rent, but it was the exposed flesh of the Dust Riders, Oxen clan, Copper Vixens, and even the Iron Guard that took the brunt of the bullets.

Whatever good the Resistance forces and its many reinforcements had done on the battlefield, halting the landships and Moving Castles of the enemy, was undone in moments once the Behemoths arrived. These monsters of machines could not be halted or chased away, and what little damage was done to them with turret fire was multiplied a thousand times in reverse.

All looked grim for the Resistance, but they had another ally in the Coilhunter that the Regime had rarely faced before.

Nox sped along the battlefield in his monowheel,

aiming straight for the nearest Behemoth, dodging gunfire, evading blasts, even narrowly missing exploding shrapnel and tumbling vehicles. He zig-zagged between the iron ruins, wound his way through spreading flames, and fired one of his many rifles to clear out some other obstacle, be it metal or flesh.

He aimed straight for a half-submerged Regime landship that had been caught in the Behemoth's path. Its nose was buried in the sand, as if to hide from the battle, and its rear stood sky-high, providing the Coilhunter a makeshift metal ramp, which he rolled up and over with ease. The monowheel sailed high, just high enough to land on the thin platform extending around the middle of the Behemoth's hull. He kept rolling, swaying a little on the edge, and fired through the open hatches as he passed them, casting aside an empty rifle for another not yet emptied.

Then the Behemoth shook, even more violently than it did before, and the hull lifted up a little, seemed to seize in place, then lifted suddenly again. Then it began to turn. Nox was caught off guard, and the monowheel slipped off the edge. He had just enough time to leap from the seat, grasping the edge of the platform as his vehicle fell into the sand.

He clambered up, finding Regime soldiers coming out of doorways to tackle him, only for him to throw them off with ease. Many had tried to wrestle with him in the Wild North. In these supposedly civilised parts, they went down just the same.

He heard a loud ping behind him as a bullet bounced off the metal plating on the guitar strapped to his back. He did not even glance over his shoulder, just rested the barrel of his pistol there and fired at the attacker behind him. He heard the man's cry, and his slipping boot, and his thud into the sand below.

Then the fire came. Grates opened at various points on the Behemoth, and flamethrowers erupted through. These cast jets far longer than the fire-flingers who worked on foot, for the furnaces of the Behemoth were huge, and dozens of slaves laboured and sweated inside to keep them burning. Tankards of oil were piled high there, fuelling the many flashing flames outside.

Nox stepped back as he neared one of these grates, feeling the hot air, and shielding his eyes from the blinding burst of flame. He waited for a moment until the jet ceased, then raced across just in time before the next blast came. His long coat was edged with embers, and his eyes glittered with the reflection of the fire.

He came to another burning grate, but this one seemed to be fuelled forever, and Nox grew impatient. Yet before he could do anything, the hull of the Behemoth shook again and began its full rotation. The platform he stood upon was not part of this movement, so he did not move with the fire—the fire came towards him. The Coilhunter had just enough time to back away from the approaching flames, only to feel the heat of the vent behind him. He turned and was caught between the two shifting flamethrowers, taking a step forward to avoid the one behind him, and trying not to step into the one ahead. He could have kept this up for some time, but as the hull turned, he found the ledge was growing slimmer all the time.

"Sorry, guys," he said, taking the last remaining orb from his belt and holding it up to his face. Then he lobbed it towards the belching fire, and it cracked open, producing a dozen clockwork butterflies. Though the flames caught them, and some tumbled down like tiny comets, the others dived through the grating, sensing the movement of the soldiers inside. They released their tiny vats of noxious gas, knocking out the makers of the flame.

Yet the fire still came behind him, and he had no more pets to summon. He took his neckerchief and wrapped it around his right gloved hand, before grasping the scalding grate with it and reefing it out of its socket. It clanged off a landship below, and he clanged off the metal floor inside the small flamethrower room when he dived inside.

He stood up, did not dust himself off, but took off the wrapping and glove from his hand, revealing the tender red beneath. It was lucky that was not his good hand. He could shoot just as well with both.

He stepped over the slumbering bodies of the soldiers, and stepped on the fallen remains of a clockwork butterfly, hearing the crunch of its little cogs. He knew he could have done with more of them, but he would have to content himself with unmaking soldiers instead.

The interior of the Behemoth was bleak. The light was dim, and everything looked like black or grey metal. It made it difficult to be stealthy, as his boots clanged as he walked. The Regime must have heard him, because they came out of their rooms in force.

As he passed one opening door, he grabbed the soldier that emerged in a headlock, while firing with his pistol into the room, then down the corridor at two more men coming out of a chamber further to the right. He snapped the man's neck, then let him drop to the ground as the Coilhunter continued his stroll through.

The thuds of his boots summoned more, and then the cries and shouts and gunshots did the rest. Soldiers came out by the dozen, and half of them fell to gunfire, and the other half became a pile of broken bones in meat sacks when he finished the battle with his fists.

He emerged into a larger room, which looked like the centre of the Behemoth. Railings extended up three levels overhead, and soldiers trotted across them, racing to their stations as the battle continued to wage outside. Some of them were given new stations: standing at the edge of the rails with machine guns pointed at him.

He swiftly pulled the guitar from his back, holding it up before him, where the metal plating on the back acted as a shield. The bullets pelted off it, bouncing off in all directions. He placed the barrel of his pistol between the curve and lined up a shot, and then another, taking out the machine gunners one by one, with not a bullet wasted, while theirs littered the ground around him.

He turned one of the knobs, and a compartment opened up in the guitar, releasing a thick smoke that spread out far around him. They continued to fire into the smoke, but he had already moved. By the time it cleared, they found him on the next level, driving a fist into a chin, whacking an ear with the side of another's gun, and kicking two of them through the rails.

He released the smoke again, and was gone, only to appear on the third level again, though this time they were waiting. They had their guns pointed at the stairwell, and he knew they would, so he did not go up that way. He climbed a ladder on the side, and yanked at people's ankles, dragging them down, before hauling himself up to finish the rest.

He cleared out the Behemoth, level by level, room by room, until it barely moved or fired on the battlefield. Then he busted through the cockpit door, spun his two pistols, and took out both drivers at the end of the spin.

"I'll drive," he said, pushing one of the bodies out of its seat.

The controls looked complex, but he was a mechanic and a tinker. He knew how to make things, and if he could not make them, he could break them. With a few adjustments, he turned the Behemoth towards its twin, which still caused havoc for the dwindling Resistance forces below. Then he drove towards it, and watched as the two collided, and clung to his seat as the other Behemoth toppled over, rocking the earth and sending the sand fleeing.

Anyone might have thought this victory enough, but the Coilhunter knew his work was not over. He could still see the Iron Emperor on the overlook, and the Hometaker firing a missile at the Rift. The demon door was opening, and he thought all Hell might break loose.

He raced back out into the battle, leaping off a platform into the sand, tumbling in place, his guitar strumming off the grains. An Oxen clan biker drove slowly past, and Nox kicked him from his seat, before hopping on instead. It was not nice, he knew, but those bikers hated him anyway.

He drove on, until he passed by the toppled monowheel, and decided he would upgrade. He abandoned the bike and pulled the monowheel up. He had barely sat down when his eyes caught a mass forming at the top of the dunes. To his great shock, these were not mere reinforcements for the Regime. They came without weapons, for these were not soldiers. They were citizens.

There were hundreds of them, and it seemed that there were hundreds more trekking across the desert to defend their Iron Empire. They were fanatics, walking with puppeteered feet, looking out with vacant eyes, never thinking, only casting themselves like bullets into the battle.

It was a desperate ploy, and Nox thought the Iron Emperor must have feared that victory was slipping from his grasp. But it was a dangerous ploy too, for there was an unwritten code of conduct in war that kept citizens relatively safe from it all. The Regime was breaking this, and as Nox watched the hordes of hapless people come down the dunes, he thought the Resistance might have to break it too.

Chapter Thirty-five

SPRINT

The Coilhunter zipped across the sand in his monowheel, dodging debris, zig-zagging between people. It tilted down forty-five degrees, until he turned sharply again and it tilted towards the other side. At times it was almost enough for someone to reach out and grab him.

The hordes continued to flood the sandy plain, and it became more difficult to evade them, to worm up that dune like the sand snakes did. He could see the Iron Emperor's roofless warwagon cruising towards the portal, and he knew he had to stop him. That was one bounty worth more than all the others.

He accelerated, and now he started to clip people as he went. The hull tilted right into the path of the crowd, striking some of them, knocking some out, sending others tumbling. It was not intended, but it did not matter. A few bruises were worth this catch, this kill.

The screams of anger and hate from the crowd were deafening. The Iron Emperor had stirred them up real good. He had a way with people. He had a spell on them. It would be difficult to break. Nox thought he might have to break their leader's neck to do it.

He saw the warwagon sailing on. It almost seemed slow in comparison to his monowheel's dreadful dash, as if the Iron Emperor had slowed down deliberately, as if he knew he could not be caught. Nox knew that was just paranoia, a trick of the mind, but he was also starting to think that maybe the last part was true.

As he flew past, some of the maddened people clawed at him. It was like racing through a forest, with branches whipping at your face. Not that there were any forests left in Altadas. The Iron Emperor was to blame for that too. But the forest of hands and nails tore at the Coilhunter, until he found that he was swimming in people, all grabbing at him, hanging onto him, pulling out of him.

The monowheel slowed.

No, he thought. *I need speed!*

But it slowed again. The weight of all the people dragging out of his coat, tearing at his mask, hanging on to each other, climbing over one another, was too much for the vehicle. It coughed and sputtered steam and smoke, and even that was muffled as people scaled their bodies on the exhaust and engine.

Nox felt several hands grabbing his mask, and saw fingers entering his blurring vision, but through all of this he could see the Iron Emperor standing up in his warwagon and turning to look at the scene below. He was haloed by the portal, a black silhouette of majesty and might surveying the peasants in the golden fields, and smiling as he left them to it.

Then Nox saw the sky, and he realised he was tumbling from his seat. The people hauled him from his vessel, dragging him down the dune, pulling him into the melee of hands and fists and frenzied faces. He was buried beneath them, like Taberah was buried deep beneath the sand, and the monowheel teetered on slowly of its own accord, without driver or passenger, stuttering as the steam began to fizzle out.

He might have been consumed by the crowd, were it not for the Iron Guard, for these new allies came to his rescue, dragging the frantic citizens one by one, casting them aside, and repeating it all again when they came back. Yet there were many fanatics on the dune, and the Coilhunter could not get away from them to pursue the Iron Emperor through the Rift.

Jacob saw the battle of bodies on the dune, and the empty monowheel, and Lorelai driving the Hometaker through the portal after the Iron Emperor. He charged towards the vehicle, leaping over a fallen zealot who tried to grab him, and hurled himself into the driving seat. He pushed down hard on the accelerator, and that dying steam came back to life.

The monowheel jolted forward, and then, to Jacob's surprise, a figure leapt at him, landing in the bucket behind him. He thought it was another manic servant of the Regime, ready to claw at him and send him tumbling just like Nox, until he heard the voice that went with it.

"Quick!" Whistler said. "They're getting away!"

Jacob stomped harder, steered faster, and ducked lower. The monowheel belched out a black cloud of smoke from the exhaust and spurred on quicker than before, as if willpower, not diesel, was its fuel.

The dune was steep, and the climb was hard, but the monowheel was gaining steam by the second. The more Jacob pushed the engine, the more it seemed to give. He did not know how Nox had made it, but he knew how to drive it, and he darted through the obstacles that sprang up periodically to halt his progress towards the Rift.

First there were stragglers from the crowd, who leapt from the top of the dune towards the approaching vehicle, rolling down towards it like boulders. Many of these were easy to dodge, but a few leapt directly at the monowheel, forcing Jacob to turn sharply left or right. What happened to these poor souls was left for Whistler to see, and he did not look behind.

Then the landships pulled out onto the dune. They parked in place, everything but their turrets, which slowly creaked around, following the fleeting black wheel that climbed the steep ascent. Jacob dived between those vehicles, skidding on sharp turns, jumping a little as they fired, smiling a lot as the shells struck the other landships across the way.

Then the moment came, and Jacob saw the portal begin to shrink.

"It's closing!" Whistler shrieked.

Jacob shook his head.

Not today, he thought. *You don't get away that easily.*

He gave it all he had, and it seemed the monowheel gave a little more. It span up the last stretch of sand, and, just as the portal seemed to flicker as it threatened to sputter out, he saw the edge of his vessel passing through. He gasped and held his breath.

There was a moment where it felt like everything froze, and even his thinking slowed. All he saw was the purple haze of the portal. He wondered for a moment if that was it, if that was where the marans lived, in some magenta void.

Then he felt a sudden jolt, and he opened his eyes, and gasped again, from both the sight and the bitter cold. It was another world all right, completely covered in ice and snow.

Chapter Thirty-six

THE COLD BLANKET

Mes Marana. They were told it was like Hell. After all, that was where the demons came from. But if this was Hell, it had frozen over.

The cold was like nothing else, and it was heightened by them coming from the immense heat of Altadas. In an older time, before the Harvest, before the invasion, this world had all but dried up. Its cracked, dusty remains had blown through the Rift into Altadas, littering its once lush soil with that now too familiar red sand. By contrast, Mes Marana was a paradise. A winter paradise.

"Here, put this on," Jacob said, taking a coat from the Coilhunter's box of second-hand goods strapped behind the monowheel's seat. It contained many things Nox had acquired from the still-warm remains of his contract killings.

Ain't no law that protects the criminal dead, the Coilhunter had croaked. *Shame to let good gear go to waste. The ground doesn't need it. The bones don't need it either.*

"I'm not wearing that," Whistler protested. "Those are dead people's clothes."

"If you don't wear this, you'll be joining them,"

Jacob replied. "You could ask their permission then, but I don't think it'd be much use." He felt he sounded harsh, but the cold was harsher.

Whistler would have kept up his petulance if the icy breeze was not so persistent. Between every word and thought, it reminded them that it was there, slowly killing them. The cold helped a little with Jacob's injuries, numbing the pain. It was about the only good it did. It created aches in the other parts that did not already ache. It seemed that the evil sun had a twin, and it was just as evil.

They tried to get the monowheel to work in the snow, but the engine would not start. What little sputters it gave only propelled the vehicle a metre or two, before it gave up the ghost again. Jacob found he was expending more effort trying to get it working than he would if they just walked instead. He did not like the idea of walking, but he did not like the idea of freezing there instead.

They journeyed for what was likely an hour, maybe two. The lack of features in this barren white landscape made it difficult to get a sense of time. There was an odd sensation in the air, and it was not just the frosty breeze. They thought they heard something else, something faint, but every time they strained to listen, it seemed to grow silent again.

In time, they had to rest, and found a small outcropping to nestle under, shielding them from the worst of the wind. Jacob managed to start a fire in one of the drier spots, and they huddled around it, shivering. What little warmth the flames gave to part of them only seemed to highlight the cold in the other parts.

"And I thought the heat was bad," Whistler complained, his teeth chattering.

"Yeah, I kind of forgot harsh winters," Jacob replied. "You wonder how they adapted."

"What do you mean?"

"How they went from this to our world."

"But wasn't ours, like … *normal* then?"

Jacob raised an eyebrow. "Yeah, I suppose it was."

"The sand came through the portal," Whistler said, looking away wistfully like he might have done when he was told about all of this. "So maybe this world was hot at first, until they abandoned it. The heat came with them, with the sand."

Jacob shrugged.

"You were there!" Whistler cried.

"Yeah, I wasn't that interested. Kind of just seemed like a big sandstorm to me. We always had sand near Blackout. I was kind of used to the desert. It was pretty much life as usual for me."

"With them invading?"

"Well, it didn't seem like an invasion, not in Blackout. It was quite a while before the war erupted properly in the east, and even then Blackout was largely immune for the first few years."

"Then it fell to them."

"Then it fell," Jacob said, "and hell, I got used to that too."

"You'd get good work in the Treasury, you know."

Jacob smiled. "Cheeky."

There was a moment where they shared smiles, meek smiles that were punctured by the probing cold.

"Thanks for not leaving me behind back there," Jacob said, rubbing a knuckle across the gash on his forehead. Both of his hands were stiff, one from the bullet wound, one from his attempts not to move the broken arm. The cold made them stiffer still. He wondered if he could even hold a gun now, and practised the gesture with a grimace.

"No problem," Whistler replied, beaming.

"I mean, not just back there, but … you know, from the start. When I got thrown into the Hold, it was just another day for me, just another job gone wrong. The worst of it, I thought, was that I wasn't going to get paid. Then I met you, and hey, my life changed *a lot*, and you know, I think it changed for the better."

Whistler blushed.

"I mean it though," Jacob said. "Everything was life as usual for me, even when the world changed, even when the war started. Because I guess nothing really meant anything to me. You got a way of changing people, kid. So, I guess, yeah … thanks, friend."

He laughed it off, feeling quite embarrassed by it all. Maybe he could blame the weather. He usually needed a full bottle of whiskey for this kind of thing, and even then he did not think he would be this mushy. He hated to think it, but he wondered if part of it was because he did not expect they would both see it through to the end. He knew he could not say *goodbye*, but at least he could be grateful for the time they had.

Whistler clearly did not know how to respond.

He seemed just as embarrassed by it all as he was, but at least he was the one getting all the praise.

"I think we're probably even," he said eventually.

"Even?"

"Well, you save me, and I save you."

Jacob chuckled. "Hey, that's a good arrangement. I won't knock it."

"Will it continue after this is all over?" the boy asked. He had asked that, in various ways, before. Jacob always gave him reassuring words, but he seemed he always doubted them. Everyone else left. Why would he stay?

"If there's an after," Jacob said. "Hey, I'm sure I'll always need saving."

Whistler smiled.

Then the cold set in again, and they almost hugged the fire. They faded off into a fitful sleep, woken periodically by the probing fingers of the storm. After a few hours, the fire faded completely, and Jacob could no longer get back asleep. Whistler dozed still, and Jacob did not want to wake him, but he knew they only had so long to live there, and he was damned if he was going to let the Iron Emperor escape. He just hoped he was not damned either way.

Chapter Thirty-seven

THE BATTLE OF
FLESH AND BLOOD

In the clock tower of Blackout, the Regime forces began their siege. The doors were well-sealed, but Camholt, who had gone by the identity of an apprentice logger for the last number of years, brought a self-made battering ram with an iron tip, and handles for four people to hold it.

The main door went down with ease. It was an old, wooden one, badly weathered, and the Resistance did not replace it to avoid drawing too much attention to the building. They did not expect the attention it was getting now.

Inside the highest room, Codex Carter continued to work on the radio equipment. He knew a bit about this, but did not have Tardo's expertise. He was not entirely sure it would be ready in time. He hated the idea that he would be blamed for it.

Then he heard the battering downstairs, and he began to think that maybe he would not have to worry for long. He checked the reinforced door leading to the main room. It was locked, but he knew it could not stand forever. He already heard the straining of the other doors below.

Gus crouched behind a trader's cart within range of the clock tower. He had to pull the hat off Porridge, because it stood up over the top, feathers and all.

"My armour!" Porridge half-whispered, half-shrieked.

"Your armour? You'll get yourself killed with that!"

He glanced over to where Tardo and Gregan prepared for their assault. They had freed Gregan with ease, thanks to a dead guard outside the prison, with his keys still in his pocket. It was one of the few things the Regime had done which worked partially in their favour.

The small force was about to strike, but it did not seem they were all on the same page. Success was all about timing. Gus just was not sure he had the right people with him for that. He tried to signal, but they looked dumbfounded. He felt increasingly like he should have poured himself a drink before all this began.

Then Gregan leapt out of his cover and fired at the two Regime soldiers guarding the battered and broken door of the clock tower. Tardo poked his head out to fire, but both of them missed. Gregan would have been riddled with bullets were it not for Gus and Porridge, who raced out just in time to blast the guards.

"That was a close one," Gregan said.

"It was only close because you rushed out."

"We can't wait around here forever."

"Guys," Tardo whispered, "someone's coming."

They heard the thunder of footsteps down the spiral staircase that wound its way inside the clock tower. Gus and his newfound team stood by the door, guns at the ready, and waited for the enemy to walk right into the barrels of their guns.

But they did not come.

Gus was about to speak when he heard a clang, and saw a grenade bouncing out to greet them. He ran and dived, and the others fled as well, before the ground quaked, and whatever was left of the door was obliterated into even smaller splinters.

The cloud of dust hid the soldier that emerged, and Gus could not hear his footsteps with the ringing in his ears. But he saw them approach, and he saw that his shotgun was out of reach. He turned to face his attacker, vowing he would not die with his back turned. He saw the barrel, and the Regime uniform, and what he thought looked like the face of Hamhart, the rival innkeeper.

"You always were resilient," Hamhart said, "but this'll put you out of business."

He cocked the rifle, but fell to a bullet from another: a golden bullet.

Gus sat up to find the Baroness standing there in the haze, her night gown blowing, her golden musket smoking. She bit open a new paper cartridge and started to load the next bullet as the others regrouped to take on several more guards coming down the stairs.

"Come along then!" Ebronah said sharply, as she entered the building without a hint of hesitation. She fired swiftly at the first guard she saw racing down, and he tumbled the rest of the way. Then she ducked under the stairs while she reloaded, giving the others a chance to kill the next two men.

"Come!" she shouted at them, stepping over—and sometimes on—the bodies littering the stairway. "We have to stop them breaching the comms room."

They followed, exchanging fire with people above, until Porridge yelped and stumbled towards the wall. He held his hand to his side, where the blood leaked through his fingers.

"I've been shot!" he bellowed, and he half-fainted.

Gus gave him a light slap on the cheek and pulled him back to his feet.

"Oh God," Porridge cried, "I knew I should've worn red."

"You'll be fine," Gus told him.

"I'm seeing stars, Gus! Stars!"

"You'll be fine!"

They continued up, without any time to halt or tend their wounds, with Porridge vengefully launching several more rounds at the men above. Chunks of the stairway broke apart from the blasts, and left gaping holes for them to traverse when they climbed a little further.

Then they came to a landing about halfway up, where the Regime were waiting in force. There were many familiar faces there, people you would see running grocers, lighting lamps—people you trusted. The Resistance troops barely got a good look at them before the bullets came.

Ebronah ducked down to avoid some, one slicing

through the bundle of her hair, freeing strands that fell down to her face. The others trundled back down too, except for Gus, who was most in the line of fire. He was struck in the stomach and chest and shoulder, each forcing him back a little towards the stairs. Yet he stood strong and roared out his pain, and blasted the man on his right—that overly polite florist—and blasted the man on his left—that chimney sweeper who always left soot on the furniture, and turned his gun on the two others in the centre.

They fired at him. He took another hit, and this was one too many. He grunted and coughed, then slipped on the step, and went crashing down the spiral stairs, tumbling past the others, who clung to the wall and the railings, and leaving a trail of blood behind him.

Porridge charged up, screaming, and took down the remaining two soldiers, and even took out a mouse scurrying in the corner, only stopping when he was out of ammunition and out of breath.

The others came up slowly, maybe a little frightened of him as well. Tardo put his hand on Porridge's shoulder in consolement, as if he thought he had known Gus well. Not long at all, and yet a moment shared in battle was long enough.

Then, as they prepared to tackle the next flight of stairs up to where Codex Carter worked, and the Regime rammed the door, they heard something strike the stairs, and saw another grenade bounce down the steps toward them.

They dived, and the explosion ripped a hole in the landing, through which Tardo fell. He reached out for something, but the planks gave way with him, and he would have fallen down to his death were it not for the hand of Gregan.

The others helped him up, and he dusted himself off, and thanked Gregan, and might have spoken a thousand words of praise were he not pressed on by the Baroness, who barked orders as if they were by royal decree.

They crept up the remaining flight, and gunned down the soldiers there, including the baker Erswell and the logger Camholt, whose improvised ram had left a huge dent in the final door.

The battle was over, and there were bodies everywhere, but Gregan beckoned them to the nearby window, where they could see another group of Regime soldiers coming their way. Another battle would soon begin.

"Everything all right up there?" one of the newly-arrived soldiers shouted up.

It could not have looked all right. None of the Resistance team knew what to say, but they wanted to say it with their guns. Yet they were low on soldiers, and low on ammunition. It was the Regime's turn to storm up the stairs.

Then suddenly they heard another voice on the bottom floor of the clock tower.

"Everything is all right," it said, with a slight crackle. "This is Iron Command. Code 58766. Stay calm. Rest assured, we have everything under full control. Do not panic. Pursue your duties in the name of the Iron Emperor."

There was a shuffle of Regime salutes outside in

response, and the soldiers departed, heading to their post guarding one of the city's gates.

"What was that?" Ebronah asked.

Porridge, still clutching his soiled blouse (and the wound beneath it), hung over the bannisters, where he could see Bitnickle peeping out from under the stairs far below. It was a Regime broadcast she sent, one of many being sent out on what they thought were secure channels.

"Everything is all right," she repeated the snippet, adding a word from a different broadcast: "now."

Porridge wondered what Gus might have said, were he not lying broken on the stairs. *Better than a gun*, he might have quipped. Porridge was saddened that the innkeeper never got to see their little victory.

"Could do with more of those clockwork constructs," Gregan said.

"Never mind that," Ebronah interrupted. "We need to secure this place. Who knows how many more of them are out there."

"I'll see if I can board up the door downstairs," Tardo volunteered.

"Shouldn't you be in *there*?" Ebronah replied, pointing to the comms room.

"Me? I think I'm barred."

"I rule this city, young man. You're not barred if you can do some good in there."

She banged her fist on the door. It was almost as good as a battering ram. There was no response, but they could hear Codex Carter dragging furniture to reinforce the door.

"I'm the Grand Treasurer! Open up this instant!"

Her shrill, sharp voice could not be mimicked, and Codex Carter was reasonably reassured enough to push the furniture away and open the many locks on the door.

The room was littered with equipment, even more than Tardo had last seen it, and some of it was in piles on the floor where Codex had emptied a table to block the entrance.

"What have you done with this?" Tardo cried.

"What do you mean?" Codex responded. "I've been setting it up."

"It's a mess."

"It was a mess when I was assigned here."

"*This* is in the wrong plug for a start," Tardo said, sifting through the wires. "Ugh! This is going to take forever."

"We haven't got forever," Ebronah warned.

"How long *do* we have?"

"For all we know," she said, "we might already be too late."

Chapter Thirty-eight

IRON INIQUITY

Jacob and Whistler set out again, their teeth chattering, their legs rattling. The cold seeped into the core of them, and there it seemed to make a home. No amount of rigorous rubbing of hands or jogging on the spot could get it to leave.

The snow was similar to the sand in that it had different textures in different areas, some soft, which their feet slipped through, and others hard, packed together tight enough that it was almost solid. All of it, however, took the prints of the vehicles that had passed through, creating a trail for them to follow.

The wind picked up, and it was not the humid wind of Altadas, but an icy breeze, which swiftly turned into a snowstorm. Whistler found a pair of goggles in his borrowed coat, and he offered them to Jacob, but he refused, using his arm to guard his eyes.

At one point it seemed like they had suddenly caught up with the Iron Emperor, for there was a black silhouette ahead, barely visible in the hail. Whistler made a dash for it, and Jacob could not grab him in time. Then, as suddenly as they saw the figure enter their vision, Whistler disappeared from Jacob's. He heard the boy's yelp, and then a thud, and ran to find the snow had given way into a chasm.

Whistler groaned as he sat up, shaking the snow from his hair. He found himself in a dark chamber, still cold, but away from the deathly chill of the wind. The rocks beneath him were rough, all different shapes, knobbly even. It was only then, as his hands felt them, that his eyes caught up. They were not rocks at all. They were bodies.

He let out the most blood-curdling shriek, which echoed in the chamber, and he recoiled from the frozen faces he had touched, only to find another body beneath him, another icy hand resting on his shoulder, another arm, another leg. No matter where he moved, he stood or kneeled or crawled upon a lifeless body, perfectly preserved in the ice.

"Are you okay?" Jacob shouted down.

"No!" Whistler shouted back up at a higher pitch.

He heard a cry, then a thump, and Jacob came rolling down the slope into the chamber, landing on the corpses below. The smuggler cried out in disgust, casting an arm away from him, and glancing around until he found Whistler standing in the corner hugging the wall. He still stood on someone's torso, but only his feet touched it now.

Whistler watched as Jacob looked down at the floor with a grimace, then hopped along the bodies gingerly, trying to skip as many as possible. He reached the same wall as Whistler and placed a hand on his shoulder.

"You okay?"

Whistler shook his head. He could feel how

wide his eyes were, even though he would rather not see anything in there at all. The darkness disguised nothing. If anything, it made his eyes work harder to see the staring, frozen eyeballs of the dead.

"It's pretty grim," Jacob said.

"It's horrible!"

"Try not to panic, kid. We'll get out of here."

He looked around the entire room, while Whistler looked at the wall, resting his forehead upon it. He could still see bodies from the corners of his eyes, but did not want to close them, in case suddenly Jacob would disappear or the dead would come to life.

"Looks like the only way out of here is back where we came from," Jacob said after his brief survey. "It's steep, but I think we can climb it."

"Right," Whistler said.

"We're going to have to go back that way."

"Right."

"Over the ... you know."

Whistler took a deep breath. "I don't like this."

"I don't like it either," Jacob said, grabbing his arm. "The sooner we get it done, the sooner it's over with. Are you ready?"

"Not really."

"Let's go."

Jacob leapt out, dragging Whistler with him. As Jacob sprang, Whistler stumbled. The icy bodies made them slip. Some of them crunched. Every one of them seemed to move just a little, as if they were not quite fully dead.

To any onlooker, it was a short dash, but it felt like forever to Whistler. On reaching the entrance, he jumped eagerly onto the slope, sliding back down a little, and scampering up again so he would not feel a corpse beneath him again. Jacob pushed him up, then pulled as he got a better foothold, and the two of them scrambled out of cavern and back into the empty whiteness, where the blizzard had died down a little.

Whistler shuddered. "I want to go home."

"Yeah, remind me never to jump through portals to other worlds again. It's not half as fun as it looks."

Whistler felt the blood drain from his face, and he thought he must have looked as pale as the men and women below. He pointed ahead to where he had seen the silhouette through the snowstorm, and saw it now much more clearly. It was a mountain of bodies, at least a hundred feet high, topped with snow, but the arms and legs still stuck out, and here and there a head, some with their eyes closed, some ever watchful.

Jacob turned to see it. "Hell," he said. "This place is a graveyard."

"Can we go back to the battle?" Whistler asked, as if it would be any different back there.

"I don't know how to get back. We have to find the Hometaker."

"Are those landship tracks?" Whistler asked, pointing to the snow to their left.

"Yeah, kid. Good eyes. Looks like they're fresh too, or this storm would have covered them good."

Whistler nodded.

"What, not dashing ahead again?"

Whistler shook his head.

Jacob smiled. "I know it's creepy, but the dead can't hurt you."

"They kind of seem like they're still alive."

"That's the cold preserving them. I imagine the Iron Emperor made sure they were dead."

"He did *all* this?"

"Looks like it. Trokus said the dissidents disappeared in their thousands. Now we know where they went."

They continued on, following the trail left by the Hometaker, finding another mound of bodies ahead, and then another, until they passed half a dozen of varying sizes, and realised that this was but a fraction of the evil deeds the Iron Emperor hid from his people.

Chapter Thirty-nine

THE ALTAR OF WAR

The Hometaker was perched on a snow-capped plateau, and there was a partially broken stone altar close by. The Iron Emperor stood before it. An axe rested at his feet, and it seemed he might have used it to cleave the stone. There was no sight of his men, or of the open-top warwagon he came in, but the clue to their whereabouts could be found in the tracks that lead off the cliff, and the dent in the front of the Hometaker's hull. Lorelai stood beside the missile launcher, gun in hand. Even from a distance, she looked confused and angry.

When Jacob and Whistler spotted them, the Iron Emperor already laid his penetrating eyes upon them in return. There was no cover to be found on this blank canvas. Everything was yet to be painted, and something told them that it might be painted red.

Jacob strolled up, and Whistler hung back a little. Neither had really prepared for this. It did not look like Lorelai had either. There was an odd feeling in the air, a kind of concentration of energy at that location. Even the Iron Emperor seemed a little overcome by it, and Jacob wondered if that was why he had tried to break the altar. There were faint whispers.

"Jacob," the Iron Emperor said, stressing the name, letting the syllables slither out and trapping them between his teeth, like a snake beneath his boot, wriggling and writhing, but unable to escape.

Jacob felt seized by the word, by his name, by the power of the voice that spoke it. Yet he fought it, and tried to hide it, and felt he had to challenge back. "What do we call you?" he asked. "Doesn't even look like you have a name."

The Iron Emperor smiled. "I have a name. I have many names. But here I have a title. None of you here are worthy of calling me anything else."

Jacob ignored him, directing his attention to Lorelai. She had turned on them all, but he felt personally betrayed. He was not sure who she was now, or who she worked for. It seemed even she did not know. Yet to Jacob, all he could think was that she was a Regime spy all this time, that it had all been a lie. "Family reunion, huh?" he asked her.

She ignored him in turn. It was almost like he was not there. It was just her and the Iron Emperor. She was fully in his iron gaze.

"You never answered me," Lorelai spoke to her leader.

"You never answered me either," Jacob interjected, and she never would.

"I saw the mounds," she said.

"You saw nothing," the Iron Emperor responded.

"So many bodies."

"So much nothing."

"There were thousands of them."

"A thousand nothings."

"Will you not acknowledge it?"

"I acknowledge nothing."

There was a pause, and the whispers increased. The more the Iron Emperor spoke, the more they rebuked him. The louder they became.

"I need to know," she said. "Is there a cure? Were you ever looking?"

The Iron Emperor was clearly offended by the question. No one had asked him it before. He glanced at the altar in consternation, then turned back to Lorelai. "You doubt me?"

"It's not that I doubt you ... I just ... I need to know."

"So, you doubt me."

Lorelai's face was ashen. "It's been a long time. We still haven't found it."

Even Jacob felt the oddness now, and heard the whispers.

"And we never will," the Iron Emperor said, and it seemed like he was not quite sure why he said it. The whispers increased, until they were given a voice, and they spoke through him.

Lorelai had no words to give, and little colour in her face left to vanish.

"I made you sick, Lorelai. I made you all sick."

Still she could not respond. Her mouth and eyes were wide with horror at the thought.

"Hope is the sickness," the Iron Emperor revealed, and seemed caught by frustration in revealing it. There was a fight happening that they could not see. He was strong, but they were many. "When you first take it, thinking you are ill, it gives you the Iron

Plague. From then on, you need it, like you need me. *I* am your Hope."

Now Lorelai had some words: "Then you're also my sickness."

"You can't cure it, and you can't cure me."

"They just have to stop giving it to their young," Jacob said, "and it'll fade out in time."

"They never will. The fear is too great."

"Until they know the truth," Jacob replied.

The Iron Emperor scoffed. "There are as many truths as there are worlds, and I'll conquer every one of them. We'll mine Altadas until there is nothing left, and then we'll move on to the next one, and the next, until the very Universe bows down to me, until the stars bend in worship of the only god that ever was, and always will be. For I am War. You think you can end me, but you'll start another, and you'll find me there again, ruling you. The glory is all mine. Mine alone."

He paused and glared at Lorelai, and she was noticeably stricken by the gaze.

"Who. Am. I?" he asked, spacing out the words.

"You are our saviour."

He nodded with great satisfaction. "Do you love me?"

"Yes," she told them. It must have been a lie. It had to be.

"Do you trust me?"

"Yes." There was no way she could mean it, and yet she sounded so sincere.

"Put the gun to your head."

She put it to her head. Jacob flinched. He hoped

231

it was a ruse. He looked at Whistler, who stared back at him with worried eyes.

"Do you feel the barrel?" the Iron Emperor continued.

"Yes," she said.

"Do you feel the cold of the steel?"

"Yes," she breathed.

"Do you want to live?"

"Yes," she pleaded.

"But if I ask you, will you die for me?"

There was a moment of hesitation, but the answer was the same: "Yes."

The Iron Emperor smiled broadly. "Pull the trigger."

Jacob ran towards her, but it was too late. She fired, and she fell. The red looked starker on the snow. The sands in Altadas used to hide it a little. Not here. Here, in the maran homeworld, everything seemed to stand out.

Jacob caught Lorelai's body, and the blood splashed upon him.

"You monster!" he shouted at the Iron Emperor, and in the moment they locked eyes, Jacob felt suddenly exposed.

"No," the Iron Emperor replied. "Say it after me: *I'm the monster.*"

Jacob was surprised to find himself repeating the words. "I'm the monster."

"Good. Now get up. Leave her."

Jacob stood up, letting Lorelai drop from his arms. She was just another body now. The question was: how high would the next mound be? It could start with the three of them.

Chapter Forty

RADIO SILENCE

B rooklyn stirred. The ringing in his ears seemed to grow, like an alarm clock. It forced him to move, and the movement made him feel the sharp pain in the nape of his neck. He opened his eyes, slowly, blinking several times, to find himself in darkness. Then his eyes adjusted and he saw that he was lying on the floor of the Hometaker. He sat up and grimaced as a blinding ray of white light burned through one of the open viewports.

He heard voices outside, and glanced out to see, first, the immense bed of snow, and then the handful of figures boring bootprints into it. One of them was the Iron Emperor. There was no mistaking him and his powerful gaze, nor his commanding and hypnotising voice. Brooklyn tried not to listen too closely. He had already been controlled enough.

It took him longer than he liked to get his wits about him to realise he still had work to do. He only hoped that Lorelai's betrayal had not sabotaged that as well. He was quite surprised to find himself in Mes Marana, and quite bewildered by all the strange voices he heard, like spirit voices, machine voices, many thousands of them, all shouting and screaming.

He must have spent too long with Rommond, because part of him doubted the reality of the voices, wondering if maybe his head wound was more serious than he thought.

When he gathered his senses, he searched through the vehicle as quietly as he could, aware that at any moment Lorelai could return—or worse, the Iron Emperor himself. He was not a fighter. He had to contribute to the war effort in more subtle ways. What he tried to do would be very subtle, and one of the greatest contributions of all.

If he could find what he was looking for.

The previous flight and battle and tumble had knocked everything out of place. It was the kind of disarray that would make Rommond grumble beneath his breath, and make Brooklyn grumble a little more quietly in his soul.

He was distracted again by the spectral voices. They seemed to gather, and all of them had accusing fingers to point at the Iron Emperor. Their pleas were overwhelming, and it took a great effort for Brooklyn to block them out to focus on his mission.

Every moment of searching was valuable seconds gone, and he began to fear he might have lost his opportunity. Finally, he rummaged beneath the seats in the cockpit, feeling the handle of a large bag, and pulled it out. Inside it was radio equipment, which he connected up as quickly as he could. The antenna was already on the roof, a little buckled and bent, but still working.

He turned everything on, and listened closely. There was a lot of interference, despite how close he was. The wind worked havoc on the sound, whispering over everyone, even the spirits. But with a few adjustments and shifts in position, Brooklyn picked up the Iron Emperor's voice through the hiss.

Then he started broadcasting it. There was no one in Mes Marana to hear, bar the dead, but there were many ears in Altadas, and some were listening closely in the clock tower of Blackout.

While he let the equipment work, he began to meditate as well, and heard the spirit voices much more clearly now, and heard their attempts to force the Iron Emperor to admit what he had done to them. It was distressing when it came.

"I slaughtered them all," the Iron Emperor's voice came over the radio. "A hundred thousand, swatted like flies, for that is all they were, and ever will be. They were less than maran, less than human. I did all worlds a favour then. I got rid of the weak. And I'll get rid of more."

In Blackout, the signals came through clear and crisp.

"We've got it!" Tardo cried. He almost pulled some of the wires from the radio equipment in his excitement.

They listened, and it was unmistakable. It was the Iron Emperor, and he was incriminating himself. If his people heard what he said, there would be a rebellion like no other—unless he could get back to Altadas to hypnotise them all again.

The team at the clock tower worked swiftly to both record the conversation and start the process of taking over Regime channels to begin broadcasting on those as well. It had taken a lot of planning and effort to get to this stage. Tardo's knowledge of Regime communications was essential. Some historians might say later: in losing him, they had lost the war.

When the night was over, and the soldiers-turned-broadcasters started to fall asleep at their posts, the broadcast was put on loop, and a skeleton crew was put in place, with rotating shifts for the next forty-eight hours. The rest of them retired to their own beds, or went outside to help secure the city, or were drafted into secret meetings to discuss how things would proceed from here.

"We did it," Tardo said, relieved.

He left the clock tower building with Gregan when the first glimmers of light were emerging. Tardo was tired, but elated.

"Yeah," Gregan replied, as grumpy as ever.

Tardo could tell that he was happy too, underneath it all. He just had too much pride to show it. They had fought side-by-side on the Home Front, and won, and brought the fight to the enemy in a way they did not expect—right into the radios of their living rooms.

"And we did it together." Tardo smiled at Gregan. "Guess we can work together after all."

"Yeah, I guess we can."

They strolled down the streets of Blackout, two unlikely compatriots, united by necessity. Tardo's smile was infectious, but there was no one around but Gregan to infect. It made it easier for Gregan to slip his hand into his pocket while Tardo was not looking, and pull out a shoelace, which he swiftly lashed around the technician's neck. Tardo's cry was cut short by his choking. He struggled, trying to grasp the lace, but all he managed to do was dig his nails into his neck. The more he fought, the tighter Gregan pulled, until finally he slumped to the ground.

Gregan knelt down to where Tardo's wide-eyed face kissed the pavement, and promptly ran the shoelace through his shoe, until he tied it up tight, but not as tight as Tardo's neck. It was a snug fit, just nice. He stood up and dusted off his hands. And then he smiled, a broad and satisfied smile. Tardo's smile was definitely infectious. Gregan would be the last person he gave it to.

Chapter Forty-one

GRANTING WISHES

In Mes Marana, Jacob tried to struggle, but the Iron Emperor's voice was overpowering.

"You don't want to fight," he said.

Much of the fight in Jacob faded. It was not replaced by serenity, but by a sense of dullness.

"You don't want to resist."

The part of him that struggled seemed to pass.

"Tell me what you really want. I can grant it. I can give you anything in the world, or in the next, or in any world. I can go there. I can take you. Why fight it? Why resist? Tell me what you want."

"I want," Jacob began, and then he paused. He was not sure what he wanted. Nothing came to mind. He felt no urges, no desires, no inclinations towards anything.

"You want riches, don't you, Jacob?" the Iron Emperor taunted.

"I want riches," Jacob said, nodding.

The Iron Emperor held out his right hand, and it seemed as if there were many crates of coils there, lids open, revealing the glint of iron inside. The Iron Emperor reached inside one, lifting up a fistful of the currency, letting the coils waterfall down. There was that reassuring clink, a beat which Jacob's heart suddenly matched with a flutter.

"Good," the Iron Emperor whispered. "It's what you've always wanted." He spoke low, out of pleasure, but also to let the clink of the coils be heard.

Jacob felt compelled to move, to walk towards the treasure, to kneel down beside the chests, to reach inside, to feel that cool metal, to make again that reassuring sound. He smiled a drunken smile, and all else seemed to fade.

"Stop it!" Whistler cried.

"Why?"

"You're just playing with people's minds."

"I'm just giving him what he wants."

"No," the boy said, shaking his head frantically. "That's not who he is any more. I know. I saw it. He changed."

"People don't change, Brogan," the Iron Emperor stated.

"They do," Whistler whimpered. "They have to."

"No, they don't. They only have to obey."

"I won't obey you."

"But why?" The Iron Emperor stared at him. "Wouldn't you want a family?"

Whistler halted mid-stride and mid-pout, as if the Iron Emperor had told him to stop.

"Wouldn't you want your mother back? Wouldn't you want her to love you?"

Whistler's brow furrowed. His eyes watered. His heart panged.

"I can bring her back," the Iron Emperor promised him, like he had promised a cure.

Whistler shook his head. "Maybe you can, but you can't make her love me."

"Why not? I can do all things."

Whistler took a deep breath. "Because she already did."

This seemed to anger the Iron Emperor, as if he did not expect it, as if he did not will it.

"She *despised* you," he said.

Whistler shook his head again. The red curls—her red—caressed his face. He pointed at the Iron Emperor. "She despised *you*. Everyone does."

"The people love me."

"Only because you make them. No one feels it truly."

The Iron Emperor's chest heaved. "You know not your peril, child, to talk to me like that."

"No, but I know what I say is true."

The glare was piercing. "I will enjoy crushing you."

Whistler wanted to be defiant, to give another snappy response like Jacob would. But he was frightened. He never felt before a fear so penetrating. For the first time in his life, he felt like he had now met a real monster. The shadows continued to convulse.

"Now," the Iron Emperor said, and his smile was deathly.

Whistler tried to look away, but the voice lured him like a fish to the hook, until he found he barely noticed his head was turning. He was caught in the eyes of the Iron Emperor, those great, vast galaxies, those swirling, ever-shifting masses, the vessels of everything and nothing. They were demon eyes. Real demon eyes. He was no maran. He had hidden himself amongst them even as they had done amongst the people of Altadas. All of this was revealed in the stare. Whistler had gotten his name by spotting demons. He felt it now, that undeniable knowledge that made his belly churn.

"Pick up the gun," the Iron Emperor told him.

Whistler felt a sudden panic, as if he were drowning. The part of him in control, the real part, was being pushed down, pushed under.

He barely noticed the irritation in the Iron Emperor at having to repeat the command. "Pick up the gun."

Whistler felt the gargle, the struggle, the blackness and the helplessness. He suddenly found himself a mere occupant of his own body, watching from within, unable to stop himself from walking over to where Lorelai's corpse was, and taking up the gun.

"Good," the Iron Emperor said. "Put the barrel to your head."

Whistler complied, despite every attempt not to. He heard the whispers of the spirits a lot more clearly now, and feared it was because he would be joining them soon.

The Iron Emperor turned to Jacob. "I want you to watch."

So Jacob turned to watch, letting the snow fall from his hands. Whistler looked at him, and their eyes met, and inside each of them their trapped personas shed dry tears.

The Iron Emperor turned back to Whistler, and his smile was more menacing than ever.

"Do you feel the barrel?" he asked.

"Yes," Jacob said, and fired.

The bullet pierced through the back of the Iron Emperor's head and out of his left eye, which exploded in blood and gore. His scream was unnatural, and his shadow writhed more than ever, twisting over itself, growing a little smaller in size. He fell to his knees, and Jacob rose to his feet, his pistol in hand, with many more bullets in the barrel.

The Iron Emperor's gaze was weakened, and Jacob strolled in front of that fabled leader, that god, and blasted away his second eye. The shadow faded more, and now his voice was weak, though his wail was still otherworldly. It sounded as if now the spirits assailed him, as if his very essence was being ripped to shreds. He collapsed into a convulsing heap, his face suddenly gaunt and ghastly, his eye sockets empty and bloodied. He twisted and thrashed in place, and wriggled like a worm being devoured. And then he was still, and he cast a shadow no more.

Chapter Forty-two

REGIME RESISTANCE

In the fortress city of Ironhold in the north-east of Altadas, a place of a thousand obsidian towers, the citizens of the Regime listened attentively to their radios as they had always done, ready for the latest biased news, the next propaganda, the newest instructions on how to live their lives, how to act, how to exist, how to think. They had been trained to give those static-laced voices their fullest attention, and today was only different in the content they heard.

"I made them sick," the Iron Emperor announced, as the Resistance took over every radio channel, broadcasting straight from Mes Marana, where the evils of the Regime leader were being revealed. He knew many things, and said he knew all, but he did not know that his own people were listening.

In the Iron Palace, an obsidian pyramid topped by a giant tower, where the Iron Emperor made his dwelling, there were but a handful of guards left to patrol its long, dark halls. A woman stood in one of the corridors with a mop, polishing the same place over and over as she listened to the nearby radio.

"A hundred thousand defiers here," the Iron

Emperor said. "Who can count the thousands more on the other worlds we conquered?"

For years she had made those floors shine, in honour of the Iron Emperor, even after her husband disappeared. He had expressed disquiet over some of the Regime's policies. She had urged him to say nothing, to keep his head down, to just carry on his duties. She did not know what happened to him, and did not ask.

For years she scrubbed and polished, but now she stopped and dropped the mop with a clatter to the marble floor. A guard on the further end of the hall glanced over, and any other day he might have chased her and beat her, and made her do her duty. But he was also listening to the radio, and he also had a loved one who spoke out, then spoke no more.

In one of the Hope factories in the far east, bordering the mining town of Hopehaven, a mix of maran and human workers and slaves toiled to produce the drug that sustained them.

They too listened to the radios, which were set to channels spewing triumphant declarations of the power and majesty of the Regime. It either inspired them to become good citizens or deflated them enough to abandon any notion of resistance. Until now.

The conveyor belts continued, but the workers became slower, until eventually they stopped entirely. The guards came around, bashing some of them, shouting at others, firing warning shots into the air.

A young man looked at his arm, where the rot

of the Iron Plague had started. He had not worked fast enough and had been denied his weekly portion of Hope as punishment. A guard approached, but before he could whack the worker in the head, the man turned on him, leaping at him, knocking him to the ground.

Others followed, and more still, until the entire factory rebelled against the guards, dragging them to the ground, tearing at them, giving them all the beatings they had given out before. They seized their guns, and the worst of the guards were shot. Then the workers left the factory, guns at the ready, and poured into the mining town to take down the guards there too.

In the eastern town of Dunedale, where the most recent Iron Rally had been held, the streets were eerily quiet. The banners and streamers were still there, but there was no celebration, no festivities in the name of the Iron Emperor, the leader without a name.

In the town hall, the mayor was assembled with many of the town officials, decked out in their Regime uniforms, proudly displaying their ranks and colours. They sat around a large oval table, working out the requirements for the next rally, set to be held in two weeks' time. There were already dozens of women and children sitting at tables nearby, sewing new tapestries and flags to make the pageantry even better than the last.

The radio was on, as it always was, and they half-listened to it as they talked and worked, until that moment when the familiar voices cut out, and all they heard was the unmistakable voice of the Iron Emperor and his self-incriminating declarations.

The women stopped mid-sew, and some of the children started to cry, wondering if their missing mother or father, or older sister or brother, was among the mountains of bodies found in Mes Marana.

The mayor was flustered, standing up awkwardly. "Well," he said. "I don't know what to say."

"I do," one of the other officials said. "Some of us have had doubts before. This only confirms it all, and it's even worse than we thought. It's time we put an end to this."

Throughout all Regime territory, in the poor areas and the rich, this same pattern repeated. Cities fell and towns rose up in rebellion. The guards became the slaves, and the slaves took up their guns. The silent were given a voice, and the frightened were given courage. And those who had lived under the spell of the Iron Emperor found it suddenly broken. They stomped on his image on the coils, and tore down the posters of him, and blew up the effigies.

The pace of the rebellion would only grow in the following days and weeks as Rommond ordered dark chambers to be used to take pictures of the horrific scenes in Mes Marana, and of the Iron Emperor's dead body. Treasury balloons were used to drop leaflet bombs on Regime cities containing these further proofs, and then the newspaper offices were overrun by rebels, and they started producing broadsheets with those same images.

The headlines said it all:

THE WAR IS OVER.
THE IRON EMPIRE IS NO MORE.
THE IRON EMPEROR IS DEAD.

Chapter Forty-three

... OR GO HOME

Jacob, Whistler and Brooklyn came back through the Rift, the tribesman using the last of the Glass missiles to widen the opening again. He promised to make more, so that marans in Altadas could go and find their loved ones, and give them a proper burial.

"Spirits are calm now," he said. "It seems machine spirits were maran spirits. They sent Pilgrims too, and those of us who listen, heard. Great anger and great pain. No one there in Mes Marana to listen. It was Iron Emperor's dark secret, and might have remained so if spirits had not summoned us. He built altar there to trap them, using terrible ancient magic, long forgotten by others. His evil deed was his undoing. Hundred thousand silenced voices spoke up. Hundred thousand he thought would not stand against him ... they became an army."

"Hopefully they can rest now," Jacob replied.

"Rest? No. No rest yet until everybody knows. Still many who do not want to listen. People need to learn, and remember, so that this never happens again."

* * *

The battle was over, and so, it seemed, was the war. Some pockets of fighting would still continue throughout Altadas for some time, but as news of the Iron Emperor's death spread, Regime forces surrendered, and some commanders came to the negotiating table to discuss a truce.

Even the forces at the Dune Burrows had radios, though many of them were overcome by the Resistance before they could hear of the events in their homeworld. With the Iron Emperor gone, the fanatics on the fields stopped mid-stride and strike, bewildered, unsure of why they had leapt into battle with just their teeth and fists, unsure who they were fighting against, and who they were fighting for. It was all a blur, and it would take a long time to come to terms with it all.

Blackout was cleared out of Regime forces, and Bitnickle played an integral role in ensuring those forces knew what had transpired elsewhere. Once the news got out, many of the groups that controlled the gates gave up without a fight. You could not anger the Iron Emperor if he was dead. The Desert Hawk, on the other hand, was very much alive.

Rommond negotiated the formal terms by which the Regime surrendered, and he was generous to those who genuinely wanted an end to the bloodshed. He recognised that past treaties had incited indignation and resentment, and he wondered what he might have accepted if he had lost the war.

Yet there were some in the Regime who would not accept this turn of events, and these were often of the highest ranks, people who still remained in the

Iron Emperor's iron grip, even from beyond the grave. Some of these had ordered atrocities, and others had committed them. Many of them were attacked by their own people in the uprising that followed, dragged out into the streets and beaten, or hung in public executions, or incarcerated, or handed over to Rommond to do as he saw fit.

The general recognised the demon in some of them, and wondered if they could ever be redeemed, and then thought of the demons among his own, and knew that they could not. Little was discussed about what happened to these, for even a grave would be a problem, when there were still some—now silent, and waiting—who supported them, and who might worship their remains, and use their burial sites as a means to inspire others to find the demon in them too.

The dead were buried, and there were many of them. Some were just a name and number, with no family left to grieve for them. Others were well-known, like Mudro, that stranger from another land who fought for Altadas. Lorelai's betrayal was largely covered up, at Jacob's request, knowing how much control the Iron Emperor had exerted on her. Her body was buried in Mes Marana, where perhaps, if there was an after life, she might see her son again. The battlefields were combed for all of the dead, though some bodies would never be found. There was a new funeral every day for a long time, and the mourning continued for even longer.

Those who survived helped the other survivors, or returned to where they came from. The Coilhunter headed back to the Wild North, and grumbled when he saw that the Oxen clan biker gang was going back there too. The Copper Vixens offered their support for repairs in Blackout, and some of them settled there, while others eventually returned to the Wild North too. Gregan disappeared from Blackout, and some thought he went to that lawless land as well, and so they made sure to set a bounty for Nox to cash in on. Alex set off on an expedition into maran lands alone, excited with the prospects and the possible discoveries, hoping for something a lot less grim than Jacob and Whistler had discovered. Porridge left the city once his wound had healed and he found an outfit fitting for a grand departure. There was always much scavenging to be done, and doodads and doohickeys to find.

It would take years for the world—or worlds— to fully recover. Rationing continued for some time, and there was periodic rioting, and often old hatred sprang up anew. There would be no reparations or segregation of the population. After all, everyone looked largely the same, and Whistler could not blow the whistle on them all, and had no desire to. Integration continued, until both peoples were one, and the threat of war became a memory, albeit an important one.

Rommond headed the caretaker government for some time, aided by the Baroness, with some top representatives of the maran people in their cabinet. Then, two years later, the first elections were held, and the now retired general reluctantly agreed to stand for office, and won by a landslide, even in Copperfort, where one of Leadman's former associates ran.

The maran people continued to search for a cure, looking not now to a single charismatic leader dangling promises, but the growing field of science. Those who had once worked on weapons now toiled on means for preserving and prolonging life. The drug Hope was kept for those already infected with the Iron Plague, but newborns were not given their first dose, and so never developed the disease. In time, even if a cure was never found, the Iron Plague would fade out of existence, just like the Iron Emperor himself.

In time, a memorial was built in the Dune Burrows, and it extended through the now permanently open Rift (thanks to a constant supply of missiles from Brooklyn, and then by others whom he trained to make them), up to the very altar the Iron Emperor had died before. Lost names were found, and they were added to the marble sculptures. There was nothing more symbolic of the end of the war than the human figure in Altadas grasping the hand of the maran one in Mes Marana, an effigy that united worlds.

Chapter Forty-four

RETIREMENT

For General Rommond, the end of the war was a huge change of pace, and took a lot of adjusting to. Even before the invasion, he was a military man, and he had been in uniform since he was just fifteen years old. He could barely remember a time when he was not fighting, but though it was a major change, to him, at this stage of his life, it was a welcome one.

In his quarters in Blackout, he took a moment to look at himself in the polished mirror. His uniform was as impeccable as ever, but he could not say the same for himself. He had aged quite a bit. He could see the first tints of grey in his thick moustache, and the lines of worry and stress in his skin. War had not been kind to him, but then it had not been too cruel—after all, he was still alive.

He could feel the pistol strapped to his belt on the right side, and his revolver on the left. Normally he did not feel them. They became second nature, just another part of him, like that metal hand was to Brooklyn. Now, however, for the first time in a long time, they felt foreign to him.

He took them out, one by one, and held them up to the mirror, inspecting them, before placing them down on the dresser nearby. They made the familiar leaden sound, which normally signalled to anyone he was with at the time that the argument was over. They ended conversations like they ended lives.

He took off his cap next, revealing his well-groomed chestnut hair, also tinged with grey. Then he removed his uniform and put on civilian clothes. He could not call them "his" civilian clothes, because he had not had any for many years—indeed, many decades. He would have been forced to ask for them now from some donor, had Brooklyn not already acquired them and laid them out for him on the bed. He looked at himself in the mirror, in his shirt and trousers, tan in colour, a kind of transition from the military to the mundane. He thought he looked rather odd, but it was good to feel odd. It almost felt like being happy.

He felt lighter than he had felt in many years, free of the burden of command, free of the weight of war. He would have new worries with the task of governing, and he had to try to find a way to solve those problems without using bullets. Brooklyn's counsel would often be needed then, and always given, and always reassuring.

Rommond packed his uniform away, and wrapped his guns inside. He placed them firmly, and quite neatly, in a suitcase, and sealed it tight. He placed it aside and hoped he would never have to open it again. Brooklyn probably would have wanted him to throw it away, but a part of him felt he had to have it on hand, just in case. It would be strange, and difficult, to get up in the morning and not feel like he had to fight. He was not entirely sure what he would do.

After he had settled into his new clothes, he pulled out another case, this one filled with different supplies. This was the only case he owned that was covered in dust, and he did not like the sight of it. He wiped most of it off, and blew a cloud of it into the air, a little mushroom cloud, an explosion of time. The supplies nestled safely inside that box, like a bunker, were still pristine: small tubes of oil paint, brushes of many sizes, and a palette for mixing.

He set them aside and pulled out a blank canvas board from under the bed. He set it up by the window, where the light shone fiercely, and got to work. It felt very strange, like a memory. He was not even sure what he was painting at first, until he started to see it come together: him and Brooklyn, arm in arm, hand in hand, smiling together.

Chapter Forty-five

EVER AFTER

Jacob and Whistler spent their own retirement from duty back in Blackout, helping clean up the city, or getting in everybody's way. With no amulets left to smuggle, and no war left to fight, Jacob was out of a job, and he certainly did not see himself becoming a politician.

"So," Jacob said, kicking back on a bench in the central plaza, watching the sun go down. "They say war changes you, and they're not wrong."

"Not all for the worse though, right?" Whistler replied.

Jacob smirked. "No, not all for the worse."

"It feels weird," the boy said, "getting up in the morning and remembering the war is over."

"We've earned a rest, eh?"

"Yeah," Whistler chirped.

They stared out at the setting sun for a moment.

"Yeah, I'm bored already," Jacob said. "Not much of the sunbathing kind of guy."

"So, what then?"

Jacob shrugged. "Don't think I ever really thought this far."

"I have."

"I know *you* have. You mentioned it enough."

"Well, I guess we'll find something to do."

Jacob raised his hand dramatically as if he just had a brilliant idea. "We could start another war."

Whistler rolled his eyes at him.

"What? Kept us busy."

"I heard there's farming work north of Copperfort," Whistler suggested. "They're starting to see good rain now. Seems the weather's changing a bit now that the Rift is open for good."

"Yeah, I don't see myself milking cows, to be honest."

"You could try."

"Hey, I'll try anything, but trust me, kid … I'm not getting up that early."

"So, what do we do then?"

"I guess we help rebuild," Jacob said with not a hint of enthusiasm. He had already "helped" enough with that, and often broken things that were still intact.

"That sounds boring," Whistler replied.

"It does, doesn't it?"

Whistler worked his hat around in his hands. "What about … adventure?"

"Not had enough of that for now?"

"I think I was born in one."

"I think you're right there."

"Just … maybe something a little less dangerous."

"Hell," Jacob said, "I could go for that."

It was then that he noticed a man standing across the way, staring at them. It was a little unsettling, but then tensions were still high, and there was a large influx of people coming into the city, all of them looking for work.

The man approached, and Jacob sat up. He still had a pistol, but he did not grab it just yet. His injuries had healed, but he never quite gripped a gun the same. *They say war changes you* came to his mind again.

"You," the man said, pointing. "You're a smuggler, right?"

"Semi-retired, actually."

"As long as it's not fully retired, I don't care."

"What do you need?"

"I collect merchandise, and there's an old treasure trove up in Canyon Crescent."

Jacob furrowed his brow. "That's in the Wild North, right?"

"That's right. One of them bygone relics that ain't been touched."

"And what, you want me to touch it?"

"Two time's the charm. I want it out. Out in one piece too."

"Is it fragile?"

"No more than you are."

Jacob expected Whistler to make some cheeky comment. He glanced at him, and the boy said nothing. The merchant must have noticed the glance, because he stared at Whistler too.

"Who's the boy?" he asked, gesturing to him.

"My apprentice."

Whistler tried hard to hide his smile.

"Good," the merchant said. "You'll probably need a team for this job."

"Well, I hope you're paying for a team."

"Two thousand dollars, half up front."

Jacob smiled at the sound of the new currency that had been introduced to replace the Regime-controlled coils. "Dollars, huh? Can't get used to that."

"You'll get used to it plenty. There'll be a gold bar too, if you do it quiet."

"This isn't … illegal, is it?"

"It ain't legal *or* illegal. Ain't no one got jurisdiction there."

Jacob bit his lip. "Sounds like a grey area."

"I thought that's where smugglers liked to play."

"In the shadows, sure. How dangerous will it be?"

"Well, you get hazard pay."

"Sounding better, but that's the kind of pay you don't want to be too high a number."

"You're right there, lad. Well, the offer's on the table. Take it or leave it. I'll be in Blackout for a few days more."

"I'll consider it."

"Well, consider fast. What with all these shifting sands, everyone'll be looking to grab what they can. They'll be comin' out of the dunes! Scoundrels, the lot of them!"

What, a bit like you? Jacob thought. He had grown a little better at thinking his retorts instead of saying them. Yet, he still enjoyed a quip or two.

The merchant walked off, and the sun continued to set before them. Those who watched it often had the same realisation: that it would be back again for a new day.

"So," Whistler said in expectation.

Jacob smiled. "Guess it's time for another adventure."

About the Author

Dean F. Wilson was born in Dublin, Ireland in 1987. He started writing at age 11, when he began his first (unpublished) novel, entitled *The Power Source*. He won a TAP Educational Award from Trinity College Dublin for an early draft of *The Call of Agon* (then called *Protos Mythos*) in 2001.

He is the author of the *Children of Telm* epic fantasy trilogy and the *Great Iron War* steampunk series.

Dean also works as a journalist, primarily in the field of technology. He has written for *TechEye*, *Thinq*, *V3*, *VR-Zone*, *ITProPortal*, *TechRadar Pro*, and *The Inquirer*.

www.deanfwilson.com